THE CUMMINGS FILES

THE CUMMINGS FILES

CONFIDENTIAL

THOUGHTS ▸ IDEAS ▸ ACTIONS

DOMINIC CUMMINGS

Created by **ARTHUR MATHEWS**

faber

First published in 2020
by Faber & Faber Ltd
Bloomsbury House
74–77 Great Russell Street
London WC1B 3DA

Design by Ghost Design
Printed and bound in England by CPI Group (UK) Ltd,
Croydon CR0 4YY

A CIP record for this book
is available from the British Library

ISBN 978-0-571-36582-1

2 4 6 8 10 9 7 5 3 1

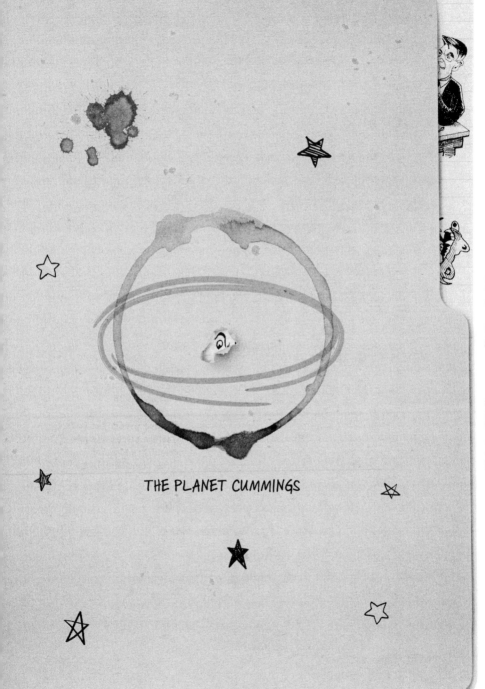

THE PLANET CUMMINGS

PAUL MASON'S
HEAD ON
PYRAMID
OF
SAUSAGES

THIS STUFF BELONGS TO:

ME

IF FOUND PLEASE ~~RETURN TO~~
BURN IT!!

DIARY

Boris has appointed me his Special Adviser. It's a momentous moment. I think now might be a good time to start writing a diary: to keep my own record of events. Campbell obviously did this, then published them after Blair died.* I don't want it to be a standard diary. I'm also keen to keep a record of my ideas, strategies and various plans and policies I like to explore: a kind of half-diary/half-blog (a 'dog' or 'bliary', one might say if one wanted to have fun with the idea – which I don't).

* Politically. He is still alive in physical form (just about – he's aged tremendously and looks awful).

The PM, at my suggestion, has also agreed that I can wear a special laminated 'thing' with my photo and name prominently displayed on it which will be on me at all times (even when I'm asleep). 'Thing' is a very vague word, but this is not a badge (which I would wear pinned to my T-shirt), nor a medal, which is often seen attached to a piece of string worn around the neck. It's like a badge on a piece of string which I can attach to myself. I actually don't think there is a word for it. Anyway, what it's called is not important. Basically, this laminated object with my photo and name on it will get me into ANYWHERE in Britain. Since we (the UK under Boris) will from now on get on just great with Trump, I expect that it will get me into anywhere in America as well. (Obviously free entry to places like the Statue of Liberty and the Grand Canyon, where I also expect I can skip the queues, but also cool joints like Studio 54. Is that still going?) Europe is much trickier, because obviously everybody there hates me and Boris.

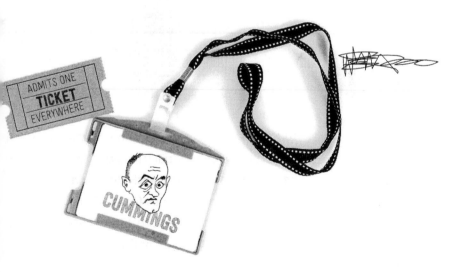

DESIGN FOR
COMMEMORATIVE MEDAL

DIARY

With Bojo in place, Brexit is basically 'done'. The whole battle with Brussels has been a tumultuous journey for both of us. I had a sit-down with the PM this morning and the discussion was most revealing. He was very candid about how he came to the pro-Brexit view: he dithered at first, really agonising about which way to go. Before deciding, he gave the issue a lot of thought. It wasn't like just introducing bendy buses in London because they looked funny. His torturous thought processes were well documented in the press, but not many people know just how forensically he went into the whole thing. He told me he wrote sixty-one essays on why Britain should leave. He then turned his brain to oppose his initial position by attempting to write some essays in favour of remaining.

I notice that when French people speak English they don't bother with trying to put on an English accent. But when the English speak French they usually have a go at the foreign accent. Can we use this???

BORIS
LION MONUMENT
(TRAFALGAR SQUARE)

Again (coincidentally, as he wasn't counting), he wrote sixty-one. He found that every argument, proposition, list of benefits and drawbacks he produced for his sixty-one pro-Leave essays was countered in his sixty-one Remain essays. (These essays, I found out later, were each a thousand pages long.) The issue was precariously balanced; his decision was on a knife-edge. Eventually, after talking to his father for an hour and a half, and then going out on the street to talk to some ordinary people, he decided to toss a coin: heads for Remain, tails for Leave. Tails it was, meaning, from that point on, he would dedicate the next few years of his life (and indeed the remainder of his entire existence) to being fervently anti-Europe. I didn't go into a similar amount of analysis. I just hate the EU. But once he'd made his mind up, it was clear we were singing from the same hymn sheet – and had the same vision for Britain. I remember last year an occasion when Varadkar and Barnier were meeting up in Brussels to try to scupper our plans for a speedy withdrawal. Boris was worried – but I told him it was basically like a play date that nine-year-olds have, where they cover each other in flour while making pancakes and then watch *Frozen* on DVD. They couldn't defeat us. They were toast. Boris smiled. He knew I was right. He trusted me.

Brexit is done. In the next election we will breach the Red Wall. The Conservative Party is vibrant. My parents have a nice house in Durham. The future is bright. Let's see what happens . . .

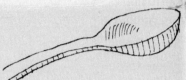

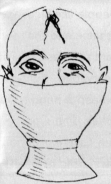

Sajid Javid came in to
the office. Seems to
know everybody's name
and I thought that
was a bit cocky. I will
BREAK him.

Summoned Nick Boles, who had been causing all kinds of trouble. Within ten minutes I had him crying like a baby. Honestly, it was like the Oscar Pistorius trial. I made it clear that there is no room for him in the party. He misheard me at first and thought I'd said 'people *like* him'. No, I'd said 'him'. He said he knew that – and that was why he had left the party in April and was now an 'Independent Progressive Conservative' (whatever that is). There'd obviously been a huge misunderstanding somewhere. I sent him on his merry way.

Later, I saw Ken Clarke in the Commons Bar. (He hates me.) He's a big jazz fan, as everybody knows. He was sounding off to a woman (didn't recognise her – probably Labour) about Ella Fitzgerald's version of 'Don't Get Around Much Anymore'. I couldn't help wondering if Ms Fitzgerald dropped the song from her set after she had to have both her legs amputated because of her diabetes.* Maybe she didn't, as it always went down well with her fans. On the other hand, she had a large repertoire to choose from, so it may not have been missed.

Is there an analogy here with Civil Service reform?

* I learnt this fact from a documentary on the BBC which was on before *Newsnight*. In general, I have little interest in jazz.

DIARY

Heard Tim Wetherspoon getting all gung-ho about Brexit on the radio. (He speaks in a funny accent because he's lived all over the place.) Great to have a seriously successful business person saying it won't be a complete disaster to leave Europe. I've been in some of his bars a few times (cheap beer for people who don't fancy the atmosphere of a traditional pub). We need more business folk to get on board. I think the pro-Brexit business community is something between zero and just over a half of one per cent. This simply isn't good enough. Even if we rounded the figures up, we'd still have just one per cent in favour of Brexit. Excluding the 'don't knows', which is just under half a per cent (also rounded down to nought per cent), that leaves ninety-nine per cent of British business against Brexit. What can we do to change this? Marx (and a younger John McDonnell) would have shot them, but I don't think that's feasible in the current climate. We'll just have to make Brexit WORK.

Brewed to 99%
proof. That should get
them going!!!

10/09 2019

BLOGPOST TO SELF

Boris believes that I am his friend. But I am not his friend. It is important that Boris believes that I am his friend. Even though I am not his friend. Gove is not my friend. Rees-Mogg is not my friend. NONE OF THEM ARE MY FRIENDS. But it is important that <u>THEY BELIEVE THAT I AM THEIR FRIEND.</u> Any notion that I could ever be friends with any of them was quickly dissipated a few years ago during the height of the idiotic 'ice bucket challenge' craze. Gove thought it would show 'the human side of the government' (Jesus!) if a few cabinet ministers accepted the 'challenge' of having a gallon (3.78541 litres) of freezing water thrown over them. One day, he bounced into Boris's office in a very jolly mood and suggested it to everybody present (me, Boris, Charles Moore from *The*

Spectator, and Daniel Craig/James Bond, who happened to be passing through). I quickly got rid of Craig and Moore, and listened to the drivel from Gove: 'Raise money for charity'; 'good for the government image'; 'a bit of a laugh'; 'shows that we don't take ourselves too seriously'. Boris thought all this was great: 'That sounds like jolly good fun, don't you think, Dom?' I let them chat to each other about this for about twenty minutes, never saying a word. About halfway through I smiled imperceptibly at a joke Boris made about Theresa May looking like someone who was in a permanent state of just having had a bucket of cold water thrown over them (a typical Boris witticism – good stuff). I knew exactly what was coming – and, predictably, it arrived just when I expected. 'Dominic! Why don't you have a go as well! Show everyone that you're game for a laugh!' Needless to say, I have never been 'game for a laugh' ever in my life. EVER. I made no response as they both looked at me nervously, waiting for a reaction. I decided to let the atmosphere sour,* as I knew it would if I said absolutely nothing. Soon the only sound in the

* Souring the Atmosphere in a Room: Techniques and Procedures by Lazlo Grypovski – a book I read when I was twelve. Some brilliant tips, obviously a huge influence on some prizewinning sourpusses, from Kissinger to Van Morrison.

room was of Gove swallowing uncomfortably and Boris struggling to twist open the cap on a bottle of ginger pop. I do have this power over them which even I find almost supernatural and 'other-worldly'. Just by doing absolutely nothing I can control them. I decided to see what would happen if I still didn't utter a word. Another half an hour passed – very, very slowly. The tension became more and more unbearable for them (but not for me, as I was utterly in command of the situation). Only when Boris, desperate to do something, took a vacuum cleaner from a cupboard and started to do some hoovering did I speak up.

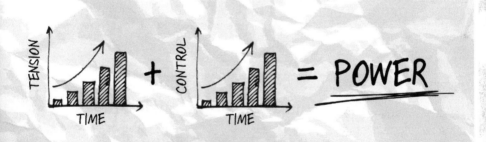

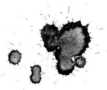

'Boris, turn off the Dyson.' He immediately obeyed. The sound of the machine faded ominously. Both he and Gove knew that when it had dwindled to silence, I would eventually speak. Both were desperately afraid by now and sweating profusely – I didn't even have to look at them; I could smell the fear. I could actually just have left the room at this point, and they would have got the message. But I didn't. I asked Boris to go outside for ten minutes, and I absolutely laid into Gove. Told him what an absurd and ridiculous idea it was for members of HM Government to have buckets of water thrown over them.

"Where's your dignity, Gove?
Where's your dignity!??"

I really let him have it, and he was fucking delighted when I told him he could leave. As he slunk off I told him, 'Send Boris in.' I wasn't as hard on Bojo, because I had given Gove such a hard time, and I was actually quite physically exhausted. But I still made it clear what I expected of him. At the end of these sessions, a sheepish Boris usually says something like, 'But we're still friends, aren't we, Dom?' I smile at him, and he usually believes this signals agreement. But it doesn't.

We can NEVER BE FRIENDS.

DECENTRALISED / PROBLEM
SOLVING / IN / ANT / COLONIES

12/09 2019

BLOGPOST: RACISM IN THE TORY PARTY

There are members of the party who just won't 'modernise'. These, of course, are the oldsters: the ones who live in the countryside, the fox hunters, the ladies who hold coffee mornings and organise tombolas (first prize: signed copy of a Jeffrey Archer novel) while their husbands read the *Racing Post* and fix themselves a comforting single-malt Glenfiddich. This is how Jeremy Corbyn, Stormzy and the BBC see Conservatives, and, regrettably, there is some truth in it. As much as I try to deny it publicly, these elderly, reactionary fossils are the backbone of the party. This is NOT GOOD.

And it is not the image we want of the Tory Party in the twenty-first century. We want . . . Grayson Perry. Perry, as I explained to Boris (who is not up to speed on popular culture), is a cross-dressing potter who makes urns featuring images of NHS nurses. He is therefore someone who is (a) likely to hate Britain and (b) unlikely to be a Tory. But my God, people love him (including my wife).

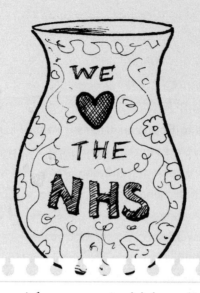

That Channel 4 programme he did during the
lockdown united bad artists all across the country
— we were treated each week to examples of their
'uplifting' (in reality, useless and substandard) work
— and I wouldn't be surprised if he got a knighthood
after all this (along with Joe, the annoying 'shout-
out' fitness guy).

Basically, we need more Grayson Perrys and fewer Godfrey Croppington-Browses. When I mentioned Croppington-Browse to Bojo, he turned a ghostly white (I know this is his normal pallor, but he definitely paled by a degree or two) and grabbed hold of the back of a nearby chair to steady himself. Luckily, Croppington-Browse (MP for Gristby North) was well gone by the time Boris became leader, but his very name still provokes fear and terror. This sad affair all kicked off under Cameron's watch during the run-up to the 2010 election. Croppington-Browse made the foolhardy (and ultimately fatal) mistake of going on Twitter without really knowing much about it. I suspect that, at the time, he was beginning to suffer from the Alzheimer's that would ultimately land him in a care home.* Although he was regularly visiting a prostitute in Leeds, his wife of many years had

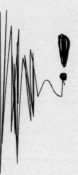

* Where, of course, he caught COVID-19 and died.

passed away during the foot-and-mouth crisis of 2001 (while trying to drag a cow from a blazing fire FULL OF BURNING ANIMALS), and he had nobody to advise him on how to deal with 'social media'. Apparently he believed that his Twitter feed would only be visible to members of the Gristby North Conservative Association. That was, unfortunately, not the case, so that when he used a swastika flag as his profile picture on the occasion of the anniversary of Hitler's birth, it is fair to say it caused a bit of a stir. News quickly spread, and we were soon treated to the familiar spectacle of a Tory MP having to furiously backtrack on national television. Croppington-Browse was forced before the cameras to issue the inevitable grovelling apology.

'I am deeply sorry if, by my irresponsible and regrettable actions, I have caused offence and distress. This was certainly never my intention. I abhor racism in all its forms, and I hope that my work for the House of Commons subcommittee on racial equality and diversity in 1998 will show that my track record on this subject is one of which I can be proud.'

Any chance of him holding on to his job disappeared when a *Guardian* journalist found one of his tweets from the week before, which stated: 'Hitler had the right idea – he should have gassed more of them!' In fact, of the twenty-three tweets Godfrey managed to post on his less-than-a-month-long flirtation with social media, twenty-one of them were deemed by the police to be 'blatantly racist'. (Five were actual 'incitements to racial hatred'.) He was, of course, soon arrested by the South Yorkshire Constabulary and was lucky to get away with community service (painting the turnstiles at York City's Bootham Crescent stadium).

CALLING OCCUPANTS OF INTERPLANETARY CRAFT email: cummings23@ woohoo.com

Sadly, Croppington-Browse is not a unique case. Every few months, three or four elderly Tory MPs are outed as reactionary racists, and it has become a major headache trying to hold back the floodgates. Of course, in years gone by, this type of thing would not have been even mildly controversial. In 1964, at their annual Christmas party, the entire Tory cabinet turned out for a

'BLACK AND WHITE MINSTRELS'-THEMED FANCY-DRESS evening and nobody even blinked an eye. In fact, the next day in the House of Commons, new Labour leader Harold Wilson

 NIGRO VITAE NON PERTINET*

congratulated the then Tory leader Alec Douglas-Home on 'what must have been a jolly and fun-filled affair'. Labour was equally culpable in very un-PC practices. At every annual TUC congress until 1980, strippers performed at the end-of-conference party, and wives were forbidden from attending (although they were allowed to set up refreshment stalls in the foyer, where they sold sandwiches and lemonade). Nowadays, they get a lecture on cultural appropriation by Ash Sarkar.

15/09
2019

DIARY

Priti Patel ran into David Icke at the post office. (Apparently he goes there every day to hand out leaflets.) I wonder . . . should I point him towards the ad I placed on the blog: 'Weirdos and Misfits'? CHECK, CHECK, CHECK, CHECK, CHECK!!!! Of course, he's mad as a hatter – but could he bring something to the party? Well, of course he couldn't, but it might be worth it just to annoy the *Guardian*. How about SECRETARY OF STATE FOR NORTHERN IRELAND? 'David, you'd be great at sorting those muck-savages out. Honestly, we really need to think outside the box on getting Stormont up and running again, and some of your stuff about lizards controlling the world might just concentrate minds.' We could actually hold a press conference and solemnly announce it. 'No, I'm not bluffing, Carole Cadwalladr.' The thing is, Carole would have no trouble at all believing that Boris would appoint David Icke to the cabinet. She'd probably get about twenty columns out of it.

Jesus, I met Boris's latest squeeze. Carrie (Carry?) Something. (All Bojo had told me about her was that 'she's obsessed with recycling plastic.')* She looks normal; could be in one of those BBC dramas wearing a sharp suit (with a skirt – is a suit with a skirt still a suit?) playing the head of Scotland Yard's antiterrorist unit. But when I started chatting to her, she came across as a full-on hippy-dippy daft. Almost immediately, after a glass of red wine (possibly organic – I didn't recognise the label on the bottle), she started nattering on about Heathrow's third runway being a shit idea. Actually, it soon emerged that she was also opposed to Heathrow's two other runways, strongly arguing they should be abolished as well... leaving Europe's busiest airport with – let's see – no runways. Would that hinder or help any post-Brexit trade deals with our new non-European friends? What do you think, Boris? NO RUNWAYS. Maybe the planes could land on Hampstead Heath or somewhere. She went to bed early and Bojo was in defensive mode. (I was PLEASED that he preferred staying up drinking with me to sex with a woman.) 'Oh, she's very committed to this stuff, but it won't influence government policy.' I made it very clear to him that that could not be allowed to happen.

* That's the weirdest hobby since Ken Livingstone raised newts to export to Iran.

BLOGPOST TO SELF

RUSSIA — people always ask me about my time in Russia. I must never respond to this. NEVER!

I must also erase the diary I kept at the time. I should resist the temptation to hold on to it for sentimental reasons or to preserve the historic record.

It's a long time ago now, and it's hard to believe that any of it happened. And yet it did. Here's what I was doing on 16 January 1995:

Reminder: I have a copy of this on a memory stick at Dad's house. Next time I visit parents I will ERASE IT!

Bezrukov and Yakusin leave tomorrow for Smolensk with the diamonds. They will meet Ovechkin and hand them over. He (Ovechkin) says the small arms, including six SR1 Vektors and a Vityaz–SN (blowback–operated Kalashnikov variant) are stored in an outhouse on Gagolin's farm. We are, however, left with the problem of Popyrin, who still refuses to talk. 'The Beast' was left alone with him for two hours last night, and when I went to the shed this morning, he was in a desperate state. I told Bezrukov to bring in a mop and wipe up the large pool of blood beside the chair, which a barely conscious Popyrin was still tied to. The Beast lives up to his name. Yakusin tells me he has been declared criminally insane by two doctors, and is an out—and—out psychopath. They (Yakusin and The Beast, whose real name I don't know) were together in Afghanistan, where The Beast was captured and badly tortured by the Taliban. It is very obvious that he has never recovered and is severely mentally unhinged. I don't know how Yakusin was able to recruit him, but he seems hugely in awe of his old army buddy and his penchant for sheer brutality. Just before he introduced him to me he said, with a mixture of fear and admiration, 'Wait till you see this guy!'

The Beast is only just over five feet in height and looks and acts like a hyperactive Siberian Charles Manson. He is an utterly vicious thug and can only be controlled by being plied with copious amounts of vodka. However, he is able to do the work that neither Bezrukov nor Yakusin are willing to do, despite the fact that they are two of the most violent hooligans I have ever met, with over forty years of jail time between them. Despite his usefulness, The Beast is an odious, unpredictable and disgusting creature, and I can't wait to see the end of him when all this is over.

THE
BEAST

I asked Bezrukov to hand me Popyrin's wallet. (Needless to say, either Bezrukov or Yakusin – or both of them together – had stolen the money from it. Each of them stands to make 500,000 roubles from this venture, but are unable to curtail their instincts as petty thieves.) I had recalled that the wallet contained a photograph of Popyrin's wife and child. I first offered Popyrin a cigarette. (I knew he wouldn't be able to accept, as The Beast had more or less sheared off his lips with a knife.) However, it was a gesture I guessed would offer him some comfort. He could no longer speak, but he was still just about able to weakly shake and nod his head. I slowly waved the photo of his wife and child in front of him. I pointed at the wife and said, 'I see that, like me, you enjoy the company of beautiful women.' I thought I detected a slight smile at this. Then I pointed at his son. 'This is your boy, is it not? He is a fine young fellow.

How old is he? Nine? Ten?' Popyrin mumbled something. It was inaudible. His voice was now nothing more than a faint whisper. I continued, 'Do you not wish to see your wife and son again? I am married myself.* I cannot imagine anything worse than being separated from my loved ones. And, of course, your family do not know where you are. They already may be fearing the worst. I am certain that they miss you as much as you miss them. You know it would be

* I wasn't.

the simplest thing in the world for you to return to them, and for all this unpleasantness to be over. All we need is one name . . . Who is Dobrynin's contact in Moscow?' There was no reaction from Popyrin. I asked him again: 'Which would you prefer? To return to your wife and child – or spend another night with The Beast?' At these words, his body went into spasm, and it looked for a moment as though he was about to break free from the ropes. He shrieked and then began crying uncontrollably. By merely mentioning The Beast's name, I had instigated complete terror in him. I then lurched forward and shouted loudly: 'WHICH WOULD YOU PREFER?!!?'** At this point he began panting very rapidly and then, soon afterwards, slumped backwards in his chair. It was clear that the interrogation would not make any further progress at this point as he was very, very weak. I told him he could take a break and consider his response. I asked Yakusin to bring him some water.***

** It's such a simple thing, but by just SHOUTING at someone, you can usually obtain the required result. I think it's a tactic that is underused. I shouted at Hancock A LOT during the early weeks of COVID-19 and always got the response I wanted.

1

2

CONVENTIONAL
(PADDLE METHOD)

MOTORIZED
(PROPELLOR DRIVEN)
IMPROVED
PERFORMANCE

*** Wow, it IS very strange reading this now. So much has happened to me in the meantime: the campaign for regional independence; the drive for Brexit; the drive to Durham; my pivotal role in leading the fight against the COVID-19 pandemic. We had to leave the dacha early the next morning as there were rumours of police in the area, and I never heard what happened to Popyrin. Likewise, I don't know where Bezrukov ended up. I do know that Yakusin rejoined the army and died in Chechnya. The Beast, not too surprisingly, became a notorious serial killer and was executed in 2001 after being captured at the end of a shoot-out with police.

GENERAL ELECTION DIARY

THE BATTLE HAS BEGUN – and we're well up for the fight. It's the old familiar story, as it's been for the last few years: it's the BBC, Channel 4, ITV, Sky, everybody who works in the arts, everybody who works in the entertainment industry, everybody who works in the publishing industry, the *Guardian*, the Civil Service, environmentalists, the Church of England, everybody who works in the NHS, Dominic Grieve and Anna Soubry against me, Boris, JEREMY CLARKSON and the ORDINARY PEOPLE OF BRITAIN. Every day someone tries to fuck us over. The newspapers report this morning that some enterprising wanker has taped an alleged 'encounter' between Boris and g'friend Carrie. This chap's a neighbour of Carrie in the tower block where she lives ('tower block' – that doesn't sound right; one thinks immediately of Grenfell Tower – I imagine it's nothing like that) and when he heard an 'altercation', he immediately got his phone out and pressed the red record button. (Surprise, surprise, it soon turns out this fellow and his girlfriend (a 'playwright') both hate Boris, think he's a fascist and a racist, and want to see Corbyn crowned king/emperor.) Anyway. Boris had called round for some red wine and hanky-panky, and as is usual in a case where men and women are involved, it ended in a huge argument. I think Boris

Will have to get 'The Beast' to pay him a visit.

was getting the brunt of it, as he's not keen on one-to-one physical confrontation. (Also, has he got fatter recently?* He might not have been able to jump out of the way.) I can imagine his line of defence – there was probably a lot of: 'Now, now, no need to start throwing the plonk around. In Ancient Greece, the Phoenicians made peace with the Egyptians by challenging them to a boulder-tossing contest.' But she screamed at him, and now it's all over the papers. I had to think fast. Get them out to Hampstead Heath or somewhere and force them to hold hands together while looking calm and reflective. Then photograph them (making it look like an opportunistic shot on an iPhone by a passing punter). Photo ends up in the *Daily Mail* and all is well again.

* I have to address this issue. Wasn't he on some fitness thing a few months ago? He certainly looked different for a while. Even his clothes looked slightly less weird on him. He should have consulted me about this.

EFFECTS OF BULLET FIRED AT RABBIT'S HEAD

GENERAL ELECTION DIARY

Was casually checking my phone when some CRAZED SCOTTISH NATIONALIST ran up to me and started berating me about something. He was pointing the finger at me (or rather, into me) for some incident – I couldn't really figure out what he was saying. Could have been about the Napoleonic Wars or the new *Star Wars* film for all I could make out. All the Scots Nats seem to swarm around Westminster with little Celtic FC holdalls slung over their shoulders as if they're prepared to spend the night on a park bench somewhere. (I think that would be bringing the independent spirit a bit far – they mostly live in flats in Pimlico.) The Scots Nats' policy in the House of Commons is one I would highly recommend: be as obnoxious, nasty, brutish and obstructive as possible, then everyone in Parliament will eventually get sick of you and be mightily relieved to see you fuck off back to Glasgow. Jesus, they're a tough lot, though. Hard as fucking nails. (Probably because of the freezing cold and general Arctic-like weather.) In Alastair Campbell's diaries, Mandelson remarked to him once when they were having a sauna together, 'Imagine if the IRA had been Scottish.' Campbell said a shiver of fear ran through both of them, and Mandelson began to sweat even more.

04/12 2019

GENERAL ELECTION DIARY

Lots of fun on the election trail. We 'rebranded' the Tory Twitter account to expose Labour's hilarious plans for lots of free stuff for everybody (money, holidays, not having to work for a living). Thought we might have got away with the annoying (unavoidable) fact that it was actually linked to the official Conservative website. (Well, we didn't really – it was fingers crossed and kind of hope that nobody would notice the tiny Tory logo in the bottom corner; but, of course, they did.) So Gove had to go face to face with some Channel 4 reporter/Tory hater who just went on and on about it.

G kept up the totally spurious pretence that it was CLEARLY linked to the official Tory website! He was quite brilliant, actually – keeping a straight face throughout. It was as if I'd somehow implanted a device in his head that kept repeating the mantra:

DON'T ADMIT IT – DON'T ADMIT IT – DON'T ADMIT IT

I've coached him over the years to just keep his head up and keep going in such trying circumstances. He's like a determined filly heading towards the finish line at the Grand National. Honestly, I even thought for a moment that he might actually have believed what he was saying.

GENERAL ELECTION DIARY

More good news: some Labour moderate has admitted to his Tory friend that Corbyn is totally useless and his party is going to get trounced in the election. All this was taped by the 'friend' (heh! heh!), and leaked to the *World at One*. Basically, Corbyn is a clown and if he wins he'll turn Britain into what Hiroshima looked like immediately after the bomb dropped. Hardly news to anybody, but great to have it on tape from someone close to the leadership. Poor Labour chap then had to go on the same show and give us the schtick that it was all 'banter' and larks. He claimed what he really believed was that Corbyn would be just great as Prime Minister, and far from turning the country to shit, it would resemble Shangri-La on a four-day week. While, yes, he had said the complete opposite on the scurrilous tape recording, he, of course, hadn't meant it. Poor guy. Having seen Gove squirming like a maggot suspended over a Bunsen burner, I had some sympathy. BUT NOT REALLY.

UPDATE ON THIS: Labour have now officially banned their members from being friends with Tories. Hah! Too late, comrades!

GENERAL ELECTION DIARY

Saw Jon Snow on College Green. The story is that he went to Glastonbury this year and was seen singing 'Fuck the Tories' with a bunch of cider-swilling crusties. (He says he doesn't recall this because he was swamped by over a thousand people asking for selfies with him.) Am I being overly suspicious of the broadcast media to think that this might just betray some political bias? Oh, I hope I'm not just being paranoid. And am I being ungenerous to Snow? Maybe when he sang 'Fuck the Tories' he was being ironic or something? I mean, it's not as if *Channel 4 News* and the BBC are run by leftists who've never had proper jobs in their lives and have come straight from universities where they've been lectured/indoctrinated by ageing Marxists/1960s hippies. I suppose maybe it's OK as long as he doesn't say it on air when he's interviewing Iain Duncan Smith or someone.

IAIN DUNCAN SMITH: 'Brexit is a definite opportunity for Britain to break free from the bureaucracy of the EU and strike out on its own.'

JON SNOW: 'FUCK THE TORIES.'

Yes, I mean, as long as something like that doesn't happen, it's probably OK.

BLOGPOST: BISMARCK

'The great issues of the day are not decided through speeches and majority resolutions, but through blood and iron.' – BISMARCK

So true. I've given this a lot of thought over the years, and I really get what the big man is saying here. (Not long after I first saw the quote, I wondered how different European history would have been if, instead of 'iron', he'd said 'irony'. I tried to imagine a twentieth century based on blood and irony. Of course, a further misspelling could have resulted in 'food and irony'. That would have been even weirder. The world as we know it might have been shaped by fat Marxist comedians.)*

* Maybe it has been?

I have never got around to finishing my screenplay about Bismarck's Kulturkampf battle against the Catholic Church in the 1870s. I saw it as ideal BBC One Sunday-night fare. Serious, like *Les Misérables* (without the songs), but also populist, like *Call the Midwife* (without the pregnancies).

CUMMINGS AS "BISMARCK"

Despite the dark subject matter, I peppered it with jokes, mostly at the expense of Pope Pius IX. Of course, the BBC would run a mile if they knew it was 'written and developed' by me, so I'd have to use a pseudonym. From what I hear, the current BBC commissioning process is frightening. I have it on good authority from an 'industry insider' what their modus operandi is these days – not that it's much of a secret anyway. According to this man, the first question they'd ask if I presented them with a Bismarck bio-series would be, 'Could the lead character be played by a woman?' In this case – no. Bismarck would be the main character – and he was a man. I think it would take quite a lot of tinkering with facts and history to turn him into a female. Ten years ago possibly Paul O'Grady (as Lily Savage) might have, at a stretch, been agreeable to both me and the BBC, but in recent years O'Grady seems to have ditched the frocks in favour of natty man-suits and now appears on screen mostly in the company of lovable dogs. However, if I managed to put them off the idea of a female Bismarck, the next conversation would certainly be about a BAME BISMARCK. I can imagine a scenario like: 'We're looking for a new vehicle for Romesh Ranganathan.' I actually enjoy Ranganathan's work, but I just don't think he'd be right. Ideally from their point of view, of course, the BBC would cast a BAME female, thus stretching credibility even further. Whatever way I look at it, I don't think my Bismarck project is going to make it at the BBC. Netflix?

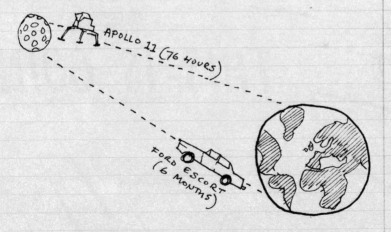

APOLLO 11 (76 HOURS)

FORD ESCORT (6 MONTHS)

DIARY – A CHAT WITH THE PM ABOUT TREACHERY

Up at Chequers to check on how Boris is getting on. (A checker goes to Chequers – this is the kind of wordplay Rees-Mogg would enjoy.) Bojo was in an untypically sombre mood, and he suggested we go for a walk. As all prime ministers do, he was moaning about the members of his cabinet. He wasn't sure that everyone was 'on message'. He stared at the ground as we sauntered through the nearby woods, hands behind his back, twiddling his fingers, moving along at a slow-to-medium pace. I would not say he was 'clearly focused' on what his plans for Britain over the next five years are, as even he admits that he makes things up as he goes along. (Although I have told him never to admit in public that he makes things up as he goes along.) As the litany of grievances unfolded, he turned to me and uttered once again those familiar words:

I hit Gove over the head with a pencil, and it broke. Not as implausible as it sounds – Gove has a small head and the pencil was quite long. Had desired result. Worth noting.

> **WHAT DO YOU THINK I SHOULD DO, DOM?**

Before giving him my answer, I suggested we tease things out for a little longer. We discussed the concept of treachery – a subject that so dogged the party during the Brexit debate. Boris mentioned Quintus Servilius Caepio the Elder, who was consul of Cisalpine Gaul during the Cimbrian War. 'He plundered the local temple and stole the legendary Gold of Tolosa.' (What was the analogy here? Something to do with Sajid Javid?) He continued to ramble on a bit, as he tends to do when musing on ancient history (a subject that fascinates us both), but at the end of the rather long story, he asked me: 'What does one do with one's enemies?' Did he mean his enemies in the cabinet? He said he did. 'Well,' I said, 'the best solution is to kill them.' He immediately burst into laughter and said, 'If only!' But I was serious. **The best solution in dealing with one's enemies is to KILL those enemies.** I could see that he was taking my suggestion seriously. But then, he blurted out: 'I can't kill Grant Shapps!' I clarified my answer. He had asked what the best solution was in dealing with one's enemies. Clearly, killing them would be the ideal solution, as they would then pose no threat to his authority. However, I had given him an 'ideal world' scenario rather than a 'real world' scenario. Of course I agreed that, while desirable, killing members of his own cabinet would not be a practical solution. 'Oh, I would really like to kill some of them, Dom!' he said, shaking his fist at a startled magpie, who flew off from a nearby branch. (He immediately apologised to the fleeing, fluttering bird.) But Boris is famously pragmatic, so, of course, murder was quickly dismissed as an option. We agreed that he should use his charm as a means of achieving consensus, and I also stressed the importance of bringing the party's whips into play. (At this point he made a funny remark about a former cabinet secretary who had a well-known penchant for flagellation.)

We retired back to the house, where Boris, in a much happier frame of mind after our chat, poured himself a glass of wine ('Domaine Dujac Clos Saint-Denis Grand Cru – rather good.') I was driving, so I declined to join him. I journeyed back to London mulling over issues of betrayal, murder and revenge. I also felt that, for one brief moment, the PM had seriously considered killing some of his cabinet members. Just because I suggested it.

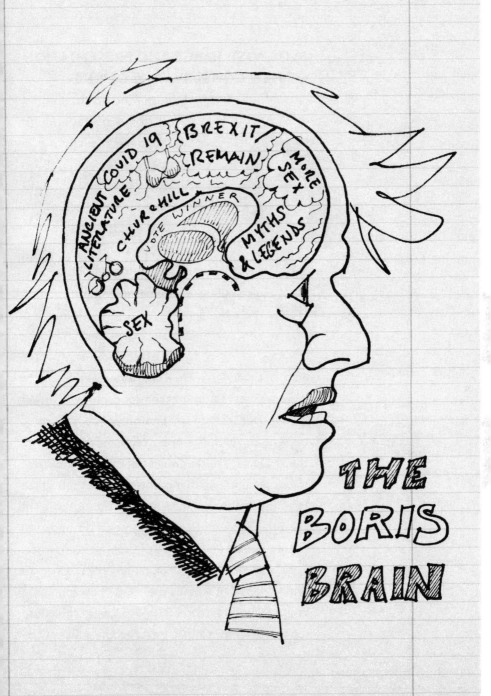

14/02 2020 · BLOGPOST: IMAGE AND PRESENTATION OF NEW CONSERVATIVE CABINET

Had a sit-down with Boris and Rees-Mogg to discuss presentation of the new cabinet. Bojo was poring over the 'official' photographs which are to be sent out with the press release. 'What do you think, Dom?' (He is always looking for approval. It can become wearying.) I remarked that Simon Hart (Secretary of State for Wales) looked a bit like Brian Clough. Rees-Mogg was a bit bemused by this, as he'd never heard of Clough. Even worse, Boris had never heard of Simon Hart. I had to remind him that he was the chap I had appointed Welsh Secretary. I forced Bojo to look at the photo for ten minutes so that he'd recognise him if the

Westminster hacks ever asked him about Hart. (Not very likely – except, of course, if they were trying to deliberately trip up the PM and embarrass him . . . which is very likely.) But Boris was pleased overall: 'Lots of diversity! Lots of BAMEs and

Must start a sweepstake: WHICH OF THEM WILL BE OUT OF THE PICTURE!!

women!' (Boris did seem hugely excited by this. I've seen him like this a lot, as if he's just pleased his teacher at prep school by doing well in an essay and has managed to avoid a beating.) Rees-Mogg was more sceptical. 'Not everything should be done to please the BBC,' he reminded the PM in a typically stern voice, his head tilted forward, eyes peering over spectacles. We proceeded to have a focused, constructive conversation as Bojo did some push-ups. He hadn't bothered to take off his jacket or shirt and tie, and to be honest it all looked a little half-hearted. He does his cycling, of course, but never goes above two miles an hour and always looks out of breath, as if he's just rushed home after having narrowly escaped being caught hiding in a cupboard by one of his mistresses' husbands.

After an hour or so, Rees-Mogg left to do some maths, and we were left alone. (Boris remarked to me after he was gone: 'I believe Rees-Mogg's wife wears a dress made out of lilacs.')

I think Boris and I do our best work when it's just the two of us in a room. Without wishing to draw an overly Nazi analogy, it's a bit like Hitler and Goebbels. Some people have said it's like Hitler and Alastair Campbell. Some others have said it's like Joachim von Ribbentrop and Ernie Wise. Whatever it is, it's a double act with a 'front man' and a 'brains'. Boris knows this and I know this. It just wouldn't work the other way around.

The Rylan

The Rolf

The Corbyn

The discussion moved on to beards (I hadn't predicted this). To be more diverse, should there be more beards in the cabinet? How representative is this of the British people? I did a quick head count and noted that the entire cabinet was clean-shaven. Allowing for the fact there are seven women in the cabinet and Gove (who is unable to grow a beard), that leaves ten men with the potential to grow facial hair, but who don't have any. I'd allocated ten minutes for this discussion, but Boris for some reason seemed determined to discuss this rather trivial subject for ever. I presumed that was because he feared that the next issue I was going

The Haddock   The Ernest   The Amish

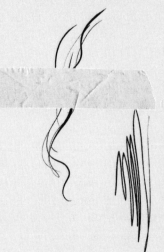

to bring up was his hair – a subject he loathes. He said that he personally feels beards (despite their popularity) are frightening and intimidating. When he was a child, the only people with beards were SEA CAPTAINS AND ROLF HARRIS, so I could broadly sympathise with his view. Often, he told me, he has to look across at the Labour benches, where beards are more plentiful amongst the Comrades. (Long tradition here, obviously: Marx, Lenin, Che, Fidel, Barry Gardiner.) 'Blunkett had one, didn't he? But at least he had the excuse that he didn't know what it looked like.' Boris's general disdain for Corbyn began to focus on his beard. 'I remember a few years ago, I was cleaning out the VC (vacuum cleaner).* The suction wasn't working properly, and I suspected that the bag was full and needed replacing. Sure enough, on lifting up the cover, I could see the bag's intake had reached the maximum level. I was right! At the time, we had a dog in the house who happened to be moulting. Its grey and brown hairs, unable to pass safely into the bag, had settled around the opening in a slimy, ghastly, revolting, tangled, matted mess . . . That's what Corbyn's beard looks like.' This observation,

* This must have been a Miele, Bojo's favourite brand until he embraced the Dyson. ('A great British product!') Dyson famously pioneered the Dual Cyclone Bagless Vacuum Cleaner, which works on the principle of cyclonic separation. (Fascinating technology at play here: I must track down a book on this subject.) In the anecdote above, the PM describes removing a dust bag, which would certainly indicate that he was using a Miele or similar product (as the Dyson is 'bagless'). I remember I was greatly intrigued when I first saw a Dyson vacuum cleaner advertised on television. It looked more like a type of robot or a futuristic weapon from *Star Wars* than a household cleaning machine. James Dyson himself (Britain's richest man or woman) was initially a strong supporter of Brexit, and the only British businessman or businesswoman apart from Tim Wetherspoon (see diary entry of 9 August 2019) who supported withdrawal from the EU. He then rather blotted his copybook somewhat by moving his headquarters from Malmesbury to Singapore. So fuck him.

honest though it was, would certainly, if raised in the House of Commons, be regarded as a highly personal attack. Tactically, I'm not in favour of this approach. Boris, of course, has faced many vicious assaults across the despatch box. I remember during the Windrush Scandal debate in 2018, Richard Burgon called him 'a blond cunt of a whore of a fucking disgrace of a cunt of a bastard'. Bercow barely raised an eyebrow.

I eventually got fed up of talking about beards and ended the meeting.

I've noticed that Boris spends a lot of his time talking enthusiastically – often at great length – about vacuum cleaners. And not just talking about them – but using them too. I've observed that when he is nervous, he will suddenly locate one in a nearby cupboard and take it out and start hoovering. I think this is partly practical: he can quite simply drown out other people's voices with the sound of the motor. But Geoffrey Cox told me that he believes the ritual originates in Bojo's long history of marital infidelities. If he'd embarked on the potentially hazardous strategy of entertaining one of his mistresses in his own house, he would habitually hoover up afterwards, vacuuming away any telltale signs of infidelity, such as earrings, lipstick holders, condoms, small bras, etc. It's a habit he apparently has found very hard to break.

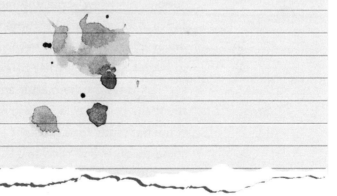

BLOGPOST: FUTURE FUNDING OF THE BBC

ANNUAL SALARIES*   * INFLATION ADJUSTED

£2,000,000

£1,000,000

£5,000

£200

£100

LINEKER   SOCRATES   HITLER   KARL MARX   CLAUDIA WINKLEMAN

Called in Oliver Dowden (Culture Minister) last week for a sit-down to discuss possible abolition of the BBC licence fee and to discuss future funding options. He knew about the meeting for a week and a half, and yet he turned up unprepared, which irritated me. (I'd never met him before, so wasn't quite sure what to expect.) I asked to hear his ideas on the matter and if he'd thought about any comparable funding models. He looked at me hesitantly for a moment – I thought he was going to cry – and then said . . . 'Argos.' Really? Argos is a soulless megastore usually located in a shopping centre where you go to browse their gigantic telephone-book-sized catalogue, select your desired product, fill in a form with a very small pen and then wait until your name is called and your children's swimming pool or curling tong is presented to you by an unhappy man or woman who hates working there. (I've always imagined they got the idea from the old East Germany.) So how would that work, Oliver? The reality, of course – and this was very obvious – was that he hadn't given it any thought at all and had just said the first thing that came into his head. I mean, what bollocks. Think about it for a moment: You'd trek all the way into your local shopping centre, go to a BBC shop (whatever that would be) and kind of 'order' programmes. It didn't make any sense at all. Dowden finally broke down and admitted that he hadn't slept a wink the night before and was 'scared' of meeting me. He'd panicked, and, for no apparent reason, once he'd stepped into my office, the word 'Argos' had started swirling around his fevered brain. What a fool.

DIARY

Hancock told me that a friend of his saw Corbyn recently in Hyde Park and he was just staring into a lake. She watched him for a full half an hour, and he just gazed into the water. (She didn't recognise him at first because he'd dyed his beard orange – like it was in the 1980s.) His eyes (very bloodshot apparently) didn't blink, and the only movement she could detect was a slight tremor in his ears. She thought she heard him humming, but it was inaudible. He was also clutching – clutching – a child's toy bow and arrow. I fucking knew he'd crack up after the election. (I wouldn't be overly surprised if he ended up in Broadmoor.) Some in Labour are now saying that he wasn't a real Socialist. If he'd been a real Socialist, they would have won. This is always Labour's excuse: 'Marx wasn't a real Socialist.' 'Lenin wasn't a real Socialist.' 'Stalin wasn't a real Socialist.' Keir Starmer apparently told Beth Rigby on *Sky News*, 'Socialism isn't real Socialism.' (He 'quickly corrected himself' and told Rigby he'd meant to say something else, but he'd suddenly felt his phone throbbing in his pocket, which distracted him.) But in Labour's view of the world to say 'Socialism isn't real Socialism' is actually consistent.

There's another book out about TRUMP. Not one of the serious ones written by a hack from the *Washington Post* or *New York Times*. One of those cheap cash-in jobs: *Words of Wisdom from Donald Trump* or something like that. Gove, who has no sense of humour and likes *Mrs Brown's Boys*, would probably say something like 'That would be a very short book!' God . . . Anyway, it's the kind of thing I'd imagine you'd see in Harry Hill's toilet alongside his BAFTA. (Not actually IN his toilet, but plonked on the floor beside it.) The Trump tome is quite high up on the bestseller list. I wouldn't be that surprised if some smart-arse somewhere is writing *The Diary of Dominic Cummings* or something similar.* (Someone like Craig Brown, but probably not as high profile). No doubt they'd have 'a lot of fun' with what's been happening over the last year – Brexit and the election and all that shit. Can I sue them? Probably not. But they're wankers nonetheless. As if they could 'get into' my mind. Even I don't know what's going on half the time.

* This is now confirmed. There was something about it in *The Bookseller*.

NEWSPAPER

TOTAL CHAOS

17/02 2020

THIS IS BULLSHIT

Bullshit, bullshit, bullshit and then you have some more bullshit followed by some more bullshit. Bull, bullshit, bullshit and then you have some more bull followed by some more.

MORE BULLSHIT

Bullshit, bullshit, bullshit and then you have some more bullshit followed by some more bullshit. Bull, bullshit, bullshit and then you have some more bull followed by bullshit.

OTHER BULL

Bullshit, bullshit, bullshit and then you have some more bullshit followed by some more bullshit. Bull, bullshit, bullshit and then you have some more bull followed by bullshit. Bull, bullshit, bullshit and then you have some more bull followed by bullshit.

DIARY

I saw another article today in the *New Statesman* which compared me to Rasputin. That's the sixth one I've seen in the last month. (Of course, one difference is that Rasputin had a lot more sex than I've had — I'm just too busy.) It's now become a habit that when I see another article comparing me to Rasputin, I immediately start singing the Boney M. song in my head ('RA, RA, RASPUTIN', not 'Rivers of Babylon' or any of their other rubbish). Gove told me that when people started calling Heseltine 'Tarzan', he began to have recurring dreams of himself swinging on a rope between trees in the jungle. He eventually had to seek counselling for it. (Apparently he had to change his first choice of therapist after she greeted him with a big smile and the words 'Hello, Tarzan!') Also, David Icke had a secretary once who, after Icke proclaimed himself Jesus, began to think that she was David Icke. It gets very interesting when you mix up mental–health issues and conspiracy theories.

SOME FAKE NEWS

Bullshit, bullshit, bullshit and then you have some more bullshit followed by some more bullshit. Bull and bullshit.

SOME MORE NONSENSE

Then you have some more bullshit followed by some more bullshit. Bull, bullshit, bullshit and then you have some more bull followed by bullshit.

Bullshit, bullshit, bullshit and then you have some more bullshit followed by some more bullshit. Bull, bullshit, bullshit and then you have some more bull followed by some more.

Bullshit, bullshit, bullshit and then you have some more bullshit followed by some more bullshit. Bull, bullshit, bullshit and then you have some more bull followed by bullshit.

Bullshit, bullshit, bullshit and then you have some bull, then you have some more bullshit, bullshit.

More bullshit followed by some more bullshit. Bull, bullshit, bullshit and then you have some more bull.

' I didn't say that '

More bullshit followed by some more bullshit. Bull, bullshit, bullshit and then you have some more bull.

More bullshit followed by some more bullshit. Bull, bullshit, bullshit and then you have some more bull.

More bullshit followed by some more bullshit. Bull, bullshit, bullshit and then you have some more bull.

MORE BULL-SHIT

Bullshit, bullshit, bullshit and then you have more bullshit followed by some more bullshit.

Bullshit, bullshit, bullshit and then you have some more bullshit followed by some more bullshit. Bull, bullshit, bullshit and then you have some more bull followed by bullshit.

Bullshit, bullshit, bullshit and then you have some more bullshit followed by some more bullshit. Bull, bullshit, bullshit and bull.

More bullshit followed by some more bullshit. Bull, bullshit, bullshit and then you have some more bull followed by some more.

Bullshit, bullshit, bullshit and then you have some more bullshit followed by some more bullshit. Bull, bullshit, bullshit and then you have some more bull followed by bullshit.

HOW DOGS FELT ABOUT BREXIT

*BASED ON OWNERS' OBSERVATIONS

DIARY

Another characteristic about Gove which I need to watch: he usually comes across as sensible and not someone who becomes overly emotional, even with the tremendous pressure he is often under; but there is another side to him, mostly hidden from the public. I remember clearly an unusual incident when we were both in the Education Dept and had travelled to Stockholm together on a fact-finding mission. We were crossing a bridge on the way to a meeting and, to my great surprise, I suddenly saw a monkey right in front of us, which possibly had escaped from a local zoo (who knows?). It had scrambled up onto the bridge rail. It didn't seem to be particularly agitated or distressed and appeared to be happily engaged in feeding itself some nuts. My plan was to notify a policeman whom I could see chatting to a member of the public about twenty metres away. But before I could suggest this to Gove, he had pushed the monkey off the bridge and into the river below. He was clearly giggling as he saw the creature fall.

I asked him. He looked up at me, trying to stifle his laughter, but then suddenly became very serious and said to me: 'Nobody must ever know about this.' Well, of course, I was never going to mention this to anyone (except to Boris, who actually loves this kind of thing and roared with laughter when I texted him about it). We never discussed the issue again, but his behaviour puzzled me at the time, and I worried that it might have been an early sign that he was suffering some kind of breakdown.

He also has a strange aversion to Malcolm Rifkind. We were talking about Rifkind once when Gove said to me, 'You know the stories about Rifkind?' I didn't understand what he meant by this, so I asked him to expand. He continued, 'They say that he paid a man to find him dead bodies.'

This seemed rather fanciful. I had never heard this rumour about Rifkind. 'Oh yes,' Gove continued. 'Where he lived in Scotland – around about this time, the early 1970s – there were a lot of unsolved murders happening in the vicinity of his castle. A strange creature had been seen in the area, and a local tradesmen had noticed it very late at night returning to Rifkind's castle. The drawbridge had been pulled up immediately after the creature had gone into the castle. Shortly afterwards, the police arrested Rifkind and charged him with harbouring a homicidal maniac.' 'Hang on a sec,' I said to Gove – because all this sounded not at all plausible, but at the same time strangely familiar – 'what you seem to be describing here is the story of Doctor Victor Frankenstein. Are you confusing Malcolm

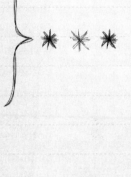

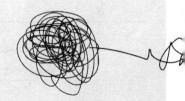

Rifkind with Doctor Frankenstein?' Gove looked thoughtful for a moment, but then replied very firmly, 'No, I don't think so – it's definitely Rifkind.' It was all nonsense,* of course, and I didn't even bother checking with the Scottish police. Was this fantasy related to a (real or imagined) rivalry that Gove had with Rifkind? Was it because they both had mild Scottish accents (Gove's to the point of practically none at all) and that they were embarrassed to be often thought of as English? It was very odd. Gove was proving to be more of a maverick than I had imagined.

* Rifkind lived in a very big house, but not a castle.

20/02 2020 BLOGPOST: PORTRAYALS OF MYSELF IN POPULAR CULTURE

A friend of my parents in Durham has had an idea which he transmitted to me through Dad. They're putting on a pantomime at Christmas (a rewrite of *Cinderella* authored by the chief sportswriter of one of the local newspapers up there – a 'bit of a wag', apparently) and one of the characters is 'Benedict Cumberbatch'. This pal of my parents wanted to know if I would like to play the role. Actually, this is quite a clever bit of potential casting, as Cumberbatch played me in that Channel 4 Brexit comedy film, so there would be a certain logic

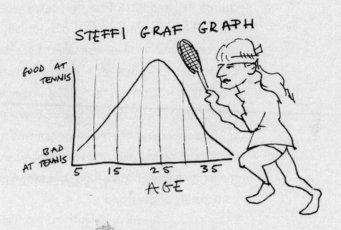

STEFFI GRAF GRAPH

GOOD AT TENNIS

BAD AT TENNIS

5   15   25   35

AGE

If the French keep their wine in wine cellars, WHERE DO Germans keep the knives **?**

to it. This man thought it would be rather a 'fun' idea. I would only have three lines (Cumberbatch is portrayed in his most famous role of Sherlock Holmes, and one of those lines is 'Elementary, my dear Watson'). Obviously rehearsals would be quite jolly as they would take place in the local church hall and lots of tea and cakes would be on offer. This unusual proposal did actually intrigue me for a time. However, it was impractical from a logistical viewpoint, as I don't wish to spend so much time in Durham (as well as undertaking the LONG AND EXHAUSTING DRIVE there and back), so my answer was no. My response was relayed to the friend of my parents, who replied that, while the pantomime group would be disappointed, they completely understood.

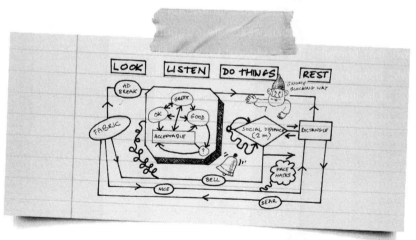

All of this made me think of how I am portrayed in the media. Not the TV or print media, where everyone thinks I'm a complete bastard, but where there are fictionalised versions of me, as in the Channel 4 Brexit comedy film. (Obviously this portrayed me as a complete bastard as well, but as a 'complete bastard with a purpose'.) As well as the inevitable 'cash-in' comedy book which I have heard is in the planning stages, no doubt *Dominic Cummings: The Musical* will also soon appear on the scene. David Steel blamed *Spitting Image* for ending his career in politics and causing his eventual suicide. There is much to contemplate here.

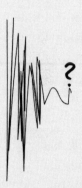

01/03
2020

BLOGPOST: FURTHER THOUGHTS ON BEARDS

I thought it might be worthwhile putting down a few more thoughts on beards, further to my intense discussion with Boris about the subject (which left both of us emotionally and physically drained). I now feel more energised and feel I can return to the subject with a less jaundiced eye. Although Brexit and Identity Politics may define this era for those of us living through it, future generations could see the late noughties and early 2020s as THE ERA OF THE BEARD.* Igor Belisokoff's book** has some very interesting things to say about this. Although written in 1955, it is probably even more relevant now than it was then. (Interestingly, I found it lying in a skip after being discarded by a homeless man.) No less than half of the work (six hundred pages) is dedicated to the 'red/ginger' or multicoloured ('salt and pepper') beard. Belisokoff gets quite angry – understandably, in my opinion – with men (and some women) who, despite having 'normal' (i.e. black, dark brown or grey hair) choose to grow a beard that turns out to be red or ginger. (He is very good on the subtle differences between the two 'hues' and explores the topic in typically forensic detail.) His basic point is: why does someone with normal hair (defined above)

* Presuming that the main visual record of the period will be from television, film, YouTube, etc., featuring numerous bearded men in various roles.

** Beards and Power: Decision-Making, Culture and Assimilation of 'The Hairy Face' in Society by Igor Belisokoff.

persist with growing a beard which they must surely know after the evidence of even a day or two (when the first ginger tufts appear) will look absolutely shit? It's bad enough having ginger hair and a ginger beard, but a ginger beard that doesn't match the hair colouring on one's head he regards as '_utterly bizarre_'. (My italics. Underlining is in Belisokoff's original text.) The Czechoslovak professor, like most people, concedes that a beard that matches hair colouring is not just acceptable but is sometimes desirable and even aesthetically pleasing. But he simply cannot understand the sheer 'lack of judgement' that is evident in the mismatched hair/beard combination. I tracked down a grainy black-and-white TV interview with Belisokoff from 1962 in which he is interviewed by Malcolm Muggeridge for the BBC's _Controversial People_ programme.

(https:www.youtube.comwatchv=8q3pac**£zz~axaa894&nn990c-nlopp7&*&&w=+yy8*8889ak3wgienbt66uiiysttsttststst777&loywy-wyw_kki90on8ytnoifwo7533)

Playing 'devil's advocate' in the studio is the bearded British actor James Robertson Justice. It is hard to tell (as the programme is in black and white) if Robertson Justice's beard is reddish in hue, but he gently chides the professor in a mostly humorous way; his charm – familiar from his role as the rogueish Sir Lancelot Spratt in the popular *Doctor in the House* series of films from the 1950s – is very much in evidence. At one point, he asks whether it is even of any importance at all if a man should choose to grow a red beard if he has black hair. 'Surely there are more pressing issues out there?' (The programme was broadcast during the time of the Cuban Missile Crisis.) 'But, you see, it is a matter of *judgement!*' roars Belisokoff in response. It becomes obvious that Muggeridge is increasingly on the side of Robertson Justice, which seems to infuriate the professor further. He eventually storms off, pulling away his microphone and calling both Muggeridge and Robertson ***** cunts.** Justice '*hajzls*'. ***

This may appear to many people as a frivolous topic, but as Belisokoff constantly states, it really is a question of judgment. Would I, for instance, trust a man (or woman) with a mismatched hair and beard to run a government department? No.

I have a slight chill.
(Seasonal flu?)
Feel a bit weird.

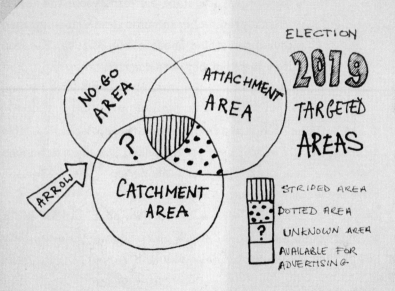

DIARY

This virus could be a real shitstorm. I thought it would be like a cold,* but the boffins are saying it will be closer to the Black Death in the 1300s, which wiped out almost everybody in the world. This is the last thing Bojo needs. I don't remember Bubonic Plague ever coming up as an election issue on the doorsteps last year, even in the north. I vaguely remember some Lib Dem virtue-signaller saying something about it, but that was because they saw a link between it and fracking.

* The last time I had a cold I cured myself through sheer determination. By willpower and concentration I actually brought my temperature down by three degrees. While shirkers – like . . . er . . . there are actually too many to mention in the Tory Party – would take to their beds for a week, my period from initial infection to complete recovery was two-and-a-half hours. So there is no way this COVID thing is going to stop me or stop Britain.

Latest figures from the experts at SAGE (scientific advisory group) suggest twenty million deaths if we do absolutely nothing about COVID (Bojo's preferred strategy). That's quite a high figure (I was expecting about fifty to a hundred). A chap called Neil Ferguson at Imperial College has

come up with some startling figures. (I haven't met him, but Hancock has. He said he literally looked like the Grim Reaper, dressed in black robes and carrying a scythe.) Ferguson stated baldly that 'something needs to be done' (he didn't specify anything in particular), or within weeks Britain

would turn into a wasteland with just a handful of
people left to bury the dead. (This is almost exactly
what we predicted would happen if Corbyn won
the election.) I googled Ferguson to find out a bit
more about him. It seems that in 2005, during the
bird flu scare of that year, he told the *Guardian*
that two hundred million people could die (final
death toll: four hundred and forty). A few years
earlier he had warned that mad cow disease could
kill fifty thousand (final death toll: one hundred
and seventy-seven). A cynic might say that since

his earlier claims were so wildly inaccurate he is therefore not the most reliable man to turn to for predictions and advice in a crisis like this. But a more generously minded person would say that, on the law of averages, he's bound to eventually get something right. Also, of course, this could be Ferguson's 'third time lucky'. So if he tells us the country is up shit creek, we should definitely listen to him. (I see also that, during the foot-and-mouth disease outbreak in 2001, he recommended that six million healthy animals be killed to stop the disease spreading. This grim process was duly carried out.* I'm hoping that he won't suggest that we kill (and burn) six million healthy UK citizens to halt this COVID thing. But if it has to be done, it has to be done.)

* See earlier note on wife of Tory MP Godfrey Croppington-Browse's attempt to rescue a cow from a huge fire.

DIARY

It's certainly not *all* bleak; nearly all of those who will die are old or frail people who contribute nothing to society. All we need to do (to keep it to just two million fatalities of old people) is to introduce 'herd immunity'. Hancock was explaining this to me the other morning: if everybody remains 'out and about' instead of staying indoors, then we'll have the whole thing sorted in a month and we can go back to the fun stuff like Brexit. The main thing is to infect each other as much as we can. This is actually great for Bojo since he's very much the 'hands-on/backslapper' type anyway. (I just find that kind of thing annoying. Gove won't like it much – he's basically a Howard Hughes type who is very, very scared of people.) When I called a cabinet meeting, I made my point VERY STRONGLY that this should be government policy. A few bed-wetters demurred – 'Oh, I've got elderly parents'... 'My wife has an underlying health condition' ... 'Why does anyone have to die?'... Fucking hell – it's called collateral damage.

THEY ARE GOING TO DIE ANYWAY!!!

It'll just be a bit sooner. If they don't die now, they'll just go next winter – when everyone will have to come back from their skiing holidays to go to the funeral.*

* Lots of old people dying could free up property which would ease the housing crisis = another +. Unless: can houses catch/be infected with the virus? Will check with Imperial College.

A COMPLETELY USELESS IDEA FROM RAAB.

He wondered if we could consider changing the name of
COVID-19 to HOVID-19, because it sounds more like 'Hovis', which
would conjure up comforting images of home-made bread.
He believes this might play particularly well in the north, where
he says they're particularly afraid of death. (Who
told him this? Eric Pickles?) I think while it's
true that when one hears the name 'Hovis' one
pictures in one's mind a cheerful baker in
the Yorkshire Dales, covered in flour and
kneading a lump of dough while his faithful
dog looks on, the reality is that the original company
became part of Rank Hovis McDougall (RHM) in 1962 after a
succession of mergers. As well as Hovis, RHM also produced the
popular Mother's Pride range. RHM was then acquired by Premier
Foods in 2007. Hovis itself became a limited company in 2014
after Premier Foods sold a fifty-one-per-cent stake in the
business to The Gores Group, the global private equity firm. So a
more appropriate image of 'Hovis' would be men in suits discussing
stock-market flotations in a large boardroom. Raab was surprised

I WILL KILL A CAT FOR YOUR APPROVAL- I WANT YOU TO LOVE ME

that I knew the history of the brand in such detail and left the room looking a little deflated. (Although I heard him mumbling something like 'I still think it's not a bad idea' on his way out.) I emailed him later saying that it was probably best to stick with the name 'COVID-19' as that had now become familiar to the public, and that if we began talking about 'HOVID-19' they'd just think we'd been struck by another pandemic. It would be confusing if it had two names. Then Rees-Mogg contacted me (no doubt after Raab had been complaining to him) to say that the thing already had two names: COVID-19 and the coronavirus. He compared it to the

Netherlands also being commonly referred to as Holland and that the names were interchangeable. This was typical Rees-Mogg bullshit (obviously informed by his pious Catholicism). There was no way that I'd allow it to be called HOVID-19 as well as COVID-19 and the coronavirus. I emailed Raab: under no circumstances was he to go on a 'solo run' on this and start using the term 'HOVID-19' on his own.

Of course, it's now leaked out that I am in favour of two million old people dying. It's as if I was Britain's biggest serial killer since Harold Shipman* (he'd have loved all this – I reckon he would probably have knocked off Britain's entire population of old folk if they hadn't caught him; he was well on the way to some kind of record). Boris was quickly on the ball: 'Oh, he didn't mean that; he was misquoted; he loves old people; his parents are in the elderly category.' It's not that I am in favour of two million people dying, but I am in favour of attaining herd immunity, which would mean that two million people would die. There is an obvious difference there. If herd immunity could be achieved without two million deaths, then great. But you can't make an omelette without breaking eggs.**

* Good newspaper headline:

'COVID-19 – GREATEST THREAT TO BRITAIN'S OLD FOLK SINCE HAROLD SHIPMAN'

** Have I just come up with this? May have heard it before somewhere . . .

Imagine if Roy Hattersley was still around. Spitting Image's portrayal of him as someone who couldn't speak without spraying everyone around him with a torrent of spit and water was cruel but hilarious. I thought of a joke I can give to a member of the cabinet to say (maybe someone like Thérèse Coffey, who needs her profile raised because no one has ever heard of her): 'Yes, Mister Speaker, but may I suggest that the Honourable Member's comments are as unpleasant as the contents of Roy Hattersley's face mask!'

DIARY

The Tory Party grass-roots, all of whom are over seventy-five, don't like the idea of all of them having to die to achieve herd immunity. Do we have another option? Called in Boris and Hancock for a brainstorming session. What are the options? I told them: sometimes it's a good idea to confuse the opposition by coming up with an idea that is IN DIRECT OPPOSITION to one's previous proposal.

Hancock was a bit perplexed by this, but Boris got it immediately. One minute, completely opposed to Brexit, the next, totally in favour of it. It's a great way to wrong-foot your opponents. So I decided we should go for the OPPOSITE of herd immunity . . . which is COMPLETE LOCKDOWN.

It was very funny to see their faces. It reminded me of George in *Seinfeld* when he's in a hopeless situation and then comes up with a terrible idea that, if anything, makes his dilemma even worse. But when he realises he has absolutely NO ALTERNATIVE, he convinces himself that, yes – THIS JUST MIGHT WORK!

Because we need THE SCIENCE behind us, I rang up Neil Ferguson at Imperial to give us his backing. He wasn't at his desk, and the phone was picked up by a cleaning lady. She said that she wasn't an epidemiologist (or indeed a scientist of any kind) but she thought that, yes, lockdown seemed like a great idea. I said that there was a possibility that she wouldn't be able to see any members of her family for at least a year, but she said she was OK with that. Great – we got exactly what we wanted: Imperial totally backs our lockdown!

24/03 2020

WAR DIARY

Everyone thinks lockdown is a brilliant idea, and the people are fully behind it. Even leftists love it, because it's the government telling them what to do. Rather brilliantly, many people have also begun to snitch on their neighbours, immediately ringing

THE SC

up the police if they see a potential troublemaker going for a 'second jog' or visiting beauty spots without written permission. Even Nazi Germany wasn't as compliant as this. I'm so pleased things are going well.

Also, importantly, we have a few more bigwigs to back us on THE SCIENCE. Boris is back from his holidays (yawning – 'What's happening with the COVID-19 thing?') and I introduced him to a brainy-looking bald man called Chris Whitty, who has a most impressive CV. He is Chief Medical Officer for England (CMO), Chief Medical Adviser to the UK government (CMUK) and Chief Scientific Adviser (CSA) at the Department of Health and Social Care. (Rees-Mogg remarked to me after we met him: 'I hope it's not a case of too many chiefs and not enough Indians.') Boris likes the idea of having boffins with loads of capital letters after their names lined up in front of him taking the flak, so when things go wrong he can blame them. As he would admit himself, he's not a man for the detail and prefers others to do the real graft (hence eight deputy mayors when he was 'running' London). He worries there may be a danger that when all of this is over, THE SCIENCE will be thanked for delivering us from the coronavirus evil and people won't be grateful enough to him. 'Like Quintus Victorius after the Battle of Placentia,' he remarked to me ruefully. 'Don't worry,' I said, 'you're going to have a great war!'

I've had lots of sit-downs with representatives of the police, NHS, etc., to drive home our lockdown message. I've seen a few visual ideas for leaflets and posters, which they've shown me, but they all seem a bit half-hearted and wimpish. Apparently, they were worried that they might overly alarm people. But that's what we want! The more alarming the better. I came up with a few ideas of my own (much superior to theirs), which will make the point more forcefully and scare people into complete submission.

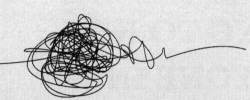

nhs.uk/coronavirus

COVID-19

IS GOING TO KILL EVERYONE IN BRITAIN

Important Information for You and Your Family

HM Government

Is your neighbour going for an unnecessary jog or making a sneaky visit to the countryside?

If so, we want to know about it.

Phone the Snoopline today:

0998 8776 9901

'You think you've got away with it? No you haven't!'

IF YOU DO NOT ADHERE TO THE TWO-METRE SOCIAL-DISTANCING RULE, YOU WILL BE HUNTED DOWN AND KILLED

'Taking lives to save lives'

STAY INSIDE FOREVER AND NEVER LEAVE YOUR HOUSE AGAIN

*Government Guidelines
on the COVID-19 Pandemic*

26/03 2020

WAR DIARY

Everything is under control and I'm actually beginning to enjoy this. There are certainly 'fun' aspects. For instance, Rees-Mogg and Iain Duncan Smith are playing Scrabble together using only words that have become popular during the crisis, such as 'hydroxychloroquine' and 'immunosuppressed'.

Rather than the three-months-to-a-year lockdown period, I think we can all probably get back to normality within a week.

They're dropping like flies! The PM, Hancock, Whitty and Alister Jack (Scotch Sec) all have it. I feel COMPLETELY SHIT so I'm presuming I have it too. Fucking hell! This afternoon I panicked a little bit and decided to run away. Unfortunately the press saw me quite clearly legging it away from Downing Street and took loads of photographs. This probably doesn't look good – me literally running away from Downing Street – so I must hold myself together. The people are looking to me to run the country during this crisis and I can't let them down.

What would Bismarck have done? During the Franco-Prussian War, could he have overseen the destruction of the French while self-isolating and working from home? I bet he could have.

Wife and child also feeling a bit under the weather. I think we need a break. Time to go on a long road trip to Durham without anyone noticing.

WAR DIARY

I like it here. We are staying in a small cottage on Dad's farm. The fields are resplendent with bluebells, and the gentle sounds of the animals and birds in the countryside are delightful to hear when I wake up in the morning with the warm spring sunshine streaming through my bedroom window. How different from the noise and clamour of London (before lockdown). All this is soothing my COVID-19 symptoms, and it's sometimes hard to believe there is a war on. This morning I danced happily and laughed in an adjacent field. Anyone looking on would have presumed I was recreating the opening scene from *The Sound of Music* with Julie Andrews.

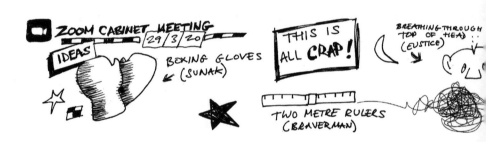

I feel I can run things just as well here as I can in the capital, through the technical wonder that is Zoom (which nobody had heard of a few months ago but which is now as essential a part of life as food and sex). I called a cabinet meeting for midday and I could see them all in their little boxes. It reminded me of that old TV show *Celebrity Squares* – except, of course, none of the cabinet are celebrities and no members of the general public would have a clue who any of them are. I think Zoom is an advantage over 'real life', as I can see all their stupid faces and they don't necessarily know which one I'm looking at. Even though their hands are usually out of shot, I know who the fidgeters and doodlers are, so I can still upbraid them if I suspect they're not paying attention. Boris, like me, is self-isolating at home (although, of course, I am not at home). Churchill spent most of World War II in bed, so I think most people will be OK with Bojo doing likewise. To be honest, he hates all this stuff anyway because it's no fun at all. There are no opportunities to meet women and he can't get out and about on his bike or go for a jog. So, all in all, it's a good time to have a little rest.

At the meeting, there was some discussion about personal protective equipment (PPE) for doctors and nurses. There isn't enough of it, apparently. I just told Raab to get some more. Raab thought Hancock was in charge of this. Then Hancock said he thought Raab was in charge. I told them to stop squabbling and just order more of the bloomin' stuff. Jesus, how simple is all this?

" JUST DO IT!!!... "

(At this point I heard an audible 'Uh!' from somebody. Did I detect a rebellious voice amongst the Zoomers? No, it turned out that Ben Wallace – defence guy – had accidentally given himself a small electric shock when he touched an exposed wire on his laptop.)

I asked if anybody else had any ideas. Rishi Sunak read somewhere that it's dangerous to touch your face with COVID in the air, as the virus can be on your hands or fingers and could then enter your body through your ears, nose or mouth. ('And anus!' chipped in Grant Shapps.) To counteract this, he thought it might be a good idea for people to wear boxing gloves.

George Eustice wondered if it might be a good idea for people to learn to breathe through the tops of their heads. For fuck's sake.

Someone called Robert Jenrick (who is he?* – will check) wondered how we were going to enforce social distancing of two metres. Everyone looked at a loss at this, until Suella Braverman, who obviously couldn't stand the awkward silence any more, suggested that every person in the country be issued with a two-metre ruler so they could accurately measure the distance between themselves and other people. Schoolchildren, now twiddling their thumbs at home with nothing to do except go on the internet to search out pornography, obviously have lots of rulers in their schoolbags, which they normally use for maths, so they could maybe join a few of these together with sticky tape to make 'two-metre rulers'. It could be a nationwide campaign, with possibly *Blue Peter* becoming involved. Perhaps Prince Charles (an actual aged COVID-19 victim himself) could personally distribute the rulers to the elderly. Liz Truss then suggested that if the ends of the rulers were fitted with a bell, it would make a noise when someone nudged the end of it as a result of breaking the two-metre cordon. Jesus Christ.

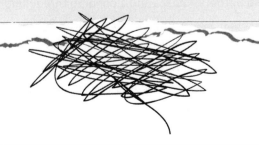

* Minister for Housing, Communities and Local Government.

WAR DIARY

Me, wife and child were feeling a bit poorly so we went to the local hospital for a check-up. Turned out we're all fine, so we went home again. (Home to the farm, that is, not London.)

The cottage and Mum and Dad's house are close to each other, but well over the recommended 'social distancing' two metres apart, so we can chat freely outdoors, even if we have to raise our voices when there is a slight breeze, or shout very loudly if there is a full-force gale.

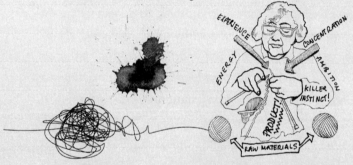

Yesterday we held a *Murder on the Orient Express*-themed (and social-distancing-friendly) barbecue for family and friends. There was no need for anybody to come in close contact with each other because a model railway had been set up, which allowed a toy locomotive and carriages to travel on a circuitous route of the property delivering burgers, kebabs and alcohol to three hundred guests. (A lovely touch was a tiny Hercule Poirot figure made of cocktail sticks, which was seated in the first-class carriage.) People simply grabbed the food and drinks off the carriages as the train chugged past slowly. It was lots of fun and everybody had a great laugh.

But it is not all fabulous here. On Tuesday I woke up in the middle of the night, suddenly remembering that there was a copy of my Russian diary on a memory stick in the garage in Mum and Dad's house, and that it was imperative that I destroy it.*

* See earlier reference to this, as well as diary extract, from 20 September 2019. (Will destroy that, too.)

OUTSIDE MY PARENTS' HOUSE I RAISED THE FIST OF MY RIGHT HAND AND YELLED OUT "DAMN YOU!"

When I looked through the window I could see and hear that there was now a full-on storm raging outside. A torrent of rain, accompanied by strong winds and thunder and lightning, was now shattering the earlier peace that I had been enjoying so much. However, I was determined to act immediately. I rushed outside in my bare feet, wearing only an old nightshirt and nightcap and carrying a candle in an old-fashioned pewter candle holder. I ran to the house and knocked loudly on the door. The rain, of course, was drenching my nightshirt and the candle had been immediately extinguished the moment I left the cottage. As I banged manically on the door, I was lit up dramatically by bright flashes of lightning. I looked up at the heavens, raised the fist of my right hand and yelled out loudly to no one in particular: 'Damn you!' (At this point the scene must have closely resembled a lavish BBC adaptation of *Wuthering Heights* and I half-expected the door to be answered by Harriet Walter or Rufus Sewell instead of my father.) But my mission was clear: I simply had to get my hands on that memory stick. When Dad finally let me in (he had been watching Joe Wicks' 'Workout for Seniors' on YouTube), I immediately sprinted through the back door to the garage and went to the box of old newspapers in which I had hidden the stick with its mass of incriminating evidence. I knew that if this was ever discovered it could very possibly land me in jail; or, in the worst-nightmare scenario, I could find myself targeted by the Russian Secret Service, like Sergei and Yulia Skripal in Salisbury.

I located the stick immediately and brought it back to the cottage, where I spent an hour bashing it to bits with a hammer. I then burned the shattered pieces in a fire. Later that morning,

AT LONG LAST!

still in my bare feet and wearing my nightshirt
and nightcap, I collected the ashes together and
threw them into a stream that divides two fields
at the back of the property. For some reason – I'm
not sure why – as I was disposing of the charred
remnants of the memory stick, I started speaking
Russian aloud. It was then that I saw a member of
the public looking at me from across the stream.
I waved at them, then walked back slowly to the
cottage.

We are running out of supplies, so I asked my niece
to go to the shop and purchase some essentials.
(I now need to replace a memory stick.)

TOILET PAPER !!!?
Fruit
Pencil
Notebook
Milk
Bread
Tomatoes
The Spectator
Memory stick

WAR DIARY

Had a long Zoom chat with Bojo, who is now in hospital. He said he felt very ill but, of course, as he admits himself, he could be lying. He was sipping orange juice and wearing his Bullingdon Club blazer over his striped pink-and-white pyjamas. (He was also, rather playfully, wearing a black wig, which one of the nurses had plonked on his head.) He was in a contemplative mood and said this period in British history reminded him of the aftermath of the Battle of the Catalaunian Plains in AD 451. He asked if I had ever seen the discussion of this battle between the historians A. J. P. Taylor and Eric Hobsbawm, where they're both obviously drunk and Taylor ends up hitting Hobsbawm over the head with a mace. (I hadn't.)

(https://www.youtube.comtaylorandhobsbawm
obviouslydrunk56662.watch?v=xZ2VicLUolRM)

He rambled on for a bit. It seems obvious that he didn't wish to discuss what exactly we're going to do about this pandemic. ('Oh, why doesn't it just go away?') I explained to him that we can't always get what we wish for. We'd all love to bring David Bowie back to life, but it's not going to happen.

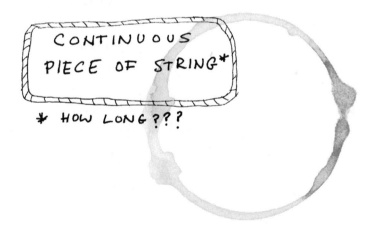

CONTINUOUS
PIECE OF STRING*

* HOW LONG???

By the end of the conversation, when he said he felt he was about to slip into a coma, I was convinced that he was faking the whole thing just so he wouldn't have to make any decisions that would make him unpopular. What a fraudster he is. With his famous charm, he'd even managed to fool the doctors into dumping him in intensive care. This was a scam he'd obviously planned so that he could become popular by sharing 'the pain of the nation'. I now (at three o'clock in the morning, after drinking heavily) sincerely believe that Britain would be much better off without him. It's generally agreed that I'm a lot more effective at running the country than he is. I even think if the roles were reversed (if he were fit and healthy and I were in intensive care) I'd still be doing a better job. Imagine . . . What would it be like if he wasn't around any more? Maybe, at this crucial time, what the nation needs is a STRONG MAN in charge? Someone new . . . A man of ABILITY and ACTION. Like Churchill in Britain's 'finest hour'. Who is that man? Is it? Could it be . . .

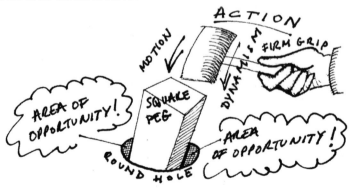

I'M VERY TIRED.

Boris is dead. Initial thoughts: I liked him but I never thought he was quite up to the job. This actually could be very positive . . . Looking back at my diary from last night —

Correction: Boris is not dead. It was Hancock playing a joke.

He said, 'Boris is dead . . .' in a text but has just followed it up with '. . . certain that he is going to get us out of this mess!' I don't think it's appropriate for Hancock to make jokes like this amid the prospect of twenty million deaths from COVID. I think you can make jokes if it's up to one hundred thousand, but after that it's not on.

Alastair Campbell notes this in his diaries: he apparently had to give John Prescott a lot of tellings-off during Blair's war on Iraq.

WAR DIARY

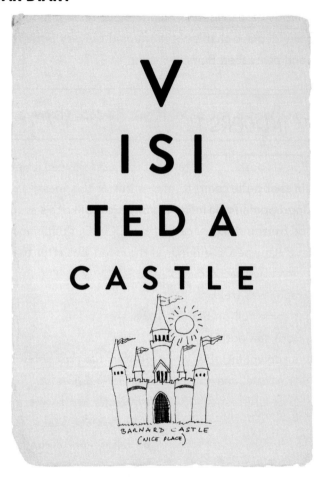

V
ISI
TED A
CASTLE

BARNARD CASTLE
(NICE PLACE)

| 14/04 |
| 2020 |

WAR DIARY

Back from our break up north and feeling healthier and much refreshed. An unremarkable trip; now looking forward to getting back to work.

WAR DIARY

It's been greatly embarrassing because Ferguson from Imperial, who suddenly decided that lockdown was the best thing for the country* and persuaded Boris that everybody in the UK should:

> " STAY INDOORS FOR AT LEAST A YEAR, "

has been breaking the 'don't go anywhere' rule so that he can shag a married woman who he is not married to (i.e. she is married to somebody else). Another point possibly worth mentioning: Ferguson has had the COVID thing as well. Apparently this lady ('blonde', 'attractive', according to the *Telegraph* and supported by photograph) was trekking across London on an almost daily basis to get some full-on biology lessons from the Coronavirus Casanova. Boris saw nothing wrong with this at all (apart from the 'breaking lockdown' bit). Bojo regards men not getting enough sex as a 'health issue', and if it were up to him he'd probably make Ferguson's type of irresponsible behaviour mandatory. But after

* Probably at the suggestion of his cleaning lady. (See diary entry of 12 March 2020.)

we discussed it for a minute or two, he did see that there was a certain amount of hypocrisy involved. 'I suppose that means he'll have to go,' he sighed. Well, of course. I then caught the beleaguered PM looking closely at the photo of Ferguson's lover in the *Telegraph*. I reckoned he was pondering whether, perhaps with the philandering professor out of the picture, he might have 'a chance' with the attractive blonde. I told him to put the paper away and get back to work.

(He's such a tosser sometimes. Obviously he's GENUINELY LAZY and HATES DOING ANY HARD WORK, but he now spends a lot of time lying on his back and staring at the ceiling. I hope he's not 'losing it' due to his alleged bout of COVID-19, which I'm still not convinced he actually had.)

I completely forgot that my trip to Durham would break lockdown rules, and now I am at the centre of a MEDIA STORM. It was a simple mistake, which anyone could have made, but now this complete non-story is all over the press and TV. Just because I was the 'architect of lockdown' and it looks very much like I broke the rules I came up with myself, I am being accused of hypocrisy. Everybody is making a huge fuss about a trip I made with my wife to a castle, the name of which I don't even remember. The reason for the visit to Barnard Castle was simple. I woke up that morning and I had gone blind. This was quite alarming, but luckily after a few hours I was suddenly able to see again. Realising that I would soon have to go on a long journey with the family back to London, I decided to do a 'test drive' to check on my eyesight. Better to go blind on a short drive along a quiet country road than to go blind at one hundred miles an hour on the M1.

BARNARD CASTLE

£1.50

58612

Luckily, the drive to the castle was uneventful. I didn't go blind and we just stopped and had a quick look around and then returned to the car. Unfortunately – and I'm very lucky that the press don't know about this – on my drive back to London, I went blind twice: once for a period of ten minutes, the second time for about fifteen minutes. In both cases, I was on a very straight stretch of road, and rather than risk stopping and pulling over, which would put both myself and my family (as well as other motorists) at risk, I decided to continue driving. Although I could see literally nothing, the road was very straight and my wife was on hand to avert any slight veering off the motorway by issuing verbal instructions ('A little to the right . . . A little to the left', etc.

As it transpired, she only had to do this on six occasions). It was all very safe and I didn't even feel there was a need at any time to reduce my speed from one hundred miles an hour, even though I couldn't see anything.

There is no question, of course, of the PM not standing by me (without CUMMINGS he knows everything would go COMPLETELY TITS UP), so I've told everyone that we all just have to sit tight and wait for this SHITSTORM IN A TEACUP to blow over.

WAR DIARY

As part of the government strategy to defend me, which I have called : **❝**

OPERATION MEDIA GO FUCK YOURSELVES **❞**

Gove had to go face to face with some Sky News/BBC reporters/ Tory haters, who just went on and on about my innocent trip to the castle. G kept to the line that it was perfectly normal to visit castles to check that you haven't gone blind, and that I hadn't done anything at all unusual. (Thank Christ he or *Sky News* or the BBC don't know that I had gone blind twice while travelling at one hundred miles an hour on my trip back to London!) Gove was quite brilliant, actually – keeping a straight face throughout. It

This little piggy went to the castle

This little piggy stayed at home

This little piggy has a future

This little piggy has none

Always wanted to have my fingerprints taken.

was as if I'd somehow implanted a device in his head that kept repeating the mantra: 'DON'T ADMIT IT – DON'T ADMIT IT – DON'T ADMIT IT'. I've coached him over the years to just keep his head up and keep going in such trying circumstances. He's like a determined filly heading towards the finish line at the Grand National. Honestly, I even thought for a moment that he might actually have believed what he was saying.

SURPRISE!!

EXPOSURE

FEAR!
(REACTION FROM CHILD)

INDOCTRINATION

WAR DIARY

Everyone is still having a fucking nervous breakdown over this. Hancock literally shat his pants at yesterday's cabinet meeting. Boris has been pacing up and down muttering, 'What are we going to do? What are we going to do?' This really pissed me off. I told him that I wished he had died of COVID-19 a few weeks ago and that he wasn't fit to be Prime Minister. Then he started crying, made another reference to an Ancient Greek battle, and went off in a sulk. I had to phone him later. I said, fuck it, to get the press to finally shut up about the whole thing, I'd hold a press conference. Bojo cheered up a bit at this, as he is totally terrified of the media and would do absolutely anything to please them. But then he got suddenly alarmed: 'You're not going to tell them to go fuck themselves or anything, are you, Dom?'

'Look,' I told him, 'they're a SHOWER OF CUNTS, but they'll only lay off this shit when they get their pound of flesh.' If they want to confront Cummings face to face, then I'm willing to do that. I have no respect for them – they're a SHOWER OF CUNTS – so it doesn't bother me that much. I might say I regret a few things to mollify them, but they know that I won't really mean anything I'm going to say.

❝Maybe you can say it with your fingers crossed behind your back?❞ (It's so typical Boris would respond like this.)

❝No, Bojo, you stupid fucker. That's something a child would do. There's no need for that.❞

❝Oh, all right then . . . Where would you like to hold the press conference? How about Wembley Stadium? There's bound to be a lot of interest!❞

It was, again, typical Boris. Loving the grand occasion but not having his eye on the bigger picture. I had to explain to him that the press conference should be limited to about two people. This was not a hard sell and he readily went along with this when I also reminded him of the two-metre distancing rule. Then I told him it would be great to hold it in the rose garden behind Downing Street. It's a nice place, with a very calming atmosphere. It's also outdoors, so easier to escape from if I absolutely had to. He immediately agreed.

WAR DIARY

Did the press conference. No big deal. It went OK. Meanwhile, a joint BBC/*Guardian* readers' poll today has named me as the most hated man in the world (of all time).

FULL CHART:

1. ↑ Cummings
2. ↓ Boris Johnson
3. Trump
4. Rees-Mogg
5. Duncan Smith
6. Douglas Murray
7. Laurence Fox (actor)
8. Farage
9. Anders Breivik (Norwegian mass killer)
10. Hitler

I don't care about it. They (the BBC and the *Guardian*) have a poll like this every few months and I'm always vying with Bojo for the number-one slot. It's like Blur and Oasis in the nineties. Boris, of course, always desperate to be liked, can't stand the fact that so many people utterly despise him. I have to remind him that the poll is not representative of everyone in the UK (if we, of course, take Scotland, Wales and Northern Ireland out of the equation). It's just *Guardian* readers, Emily Maitlis and everyone at the BBC, Jon Snow and everyone at Channel 4, Robert Peston and everyone at ITV, Adam Boulton and everyone at Sky, everybody who works in the arts, everybody who works in the entertainment industry, everybody who works in the publishing industry, the Civil Service, environmentalists, the Church of England, everybody who works in the NHS, Dominic Grieve and Anna Soubry.

GENDER PAY GAP IN ROMAN BRITAIN

CUMMINGS "ARCHITECT OF LOCKDOWN" 2020

DESIGN FOR
COMMEMORATIVE MEDAL

'But the normal people like me, don't they? All those lovely Northerners behind the Red Wall! Maybe I can even go and visit them when we get HS2 up and running!'

'Yes, they do like you,' I said. 'In fact . . . they think you're great.' His eyes lit up at this and he went off in a jolly mood to have sex.

I didn't tell him that we will have to reassess his popularity and likelihood of re-election if Hull, Manchester, Liverpool, Sheffield, etc., go up the swanny in the event that Brexit doesn't quite go like we promised them.

Anyway, all that trip-to-Durham shit is out of the way. Time to move on.

BLOGPOST: USING THE NEW MEDIA

Was watching the news last night (which I obviously hate doing, but I have to because it's my job). It was the usual round-up of depressing COVID-19 stories from around the globe. Mostly prime ministers presenting their latest litanies of woe to the weary hacks at tedious press briefings. I notice that, nowadays, in every country in the world (with the obvious exceptions of Hungary and Brazil), there is always somebody standing next to the PM doing those sign-language aerobics so that deaf people can understand what's going on. I get this. It's inclusive and empowering – all that stuff that Boris likes. But it's also a bit fucking distracting.

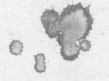

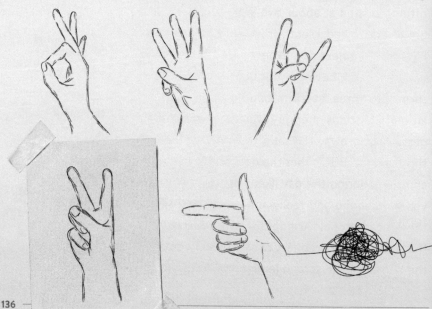

I especially dislike sign-language additions to normal TV shows. The worst thing is when I've missed a documentary about Bismarck on the BBC, which is broadcast about nine o'clock in the evening (a time when I'm usually either chairing a strategy meeting, presiding over a disciplinary hearing or being hauled before an inquiry). The programme is often repeated at about two in the morning. Just before I go to bed, I set the recording for that time. I watch it the next day, expecting it to be like the earlier version, but no – the fucking screen soon shrinks to three quarters of its normal size and an enthusiastic 'signer' is revealed in the corner, gesticulating away. (What's the thinking behind this from the BBC? That the deaf stay up at night and sleep during the day like vampires?) As I say, very distracting and really annoying – and surely the unhearing could just opt for subtitles and spare the rest of us the drudgery of watching a woman in the corner of the screen jerking her limbs wildly?

FAMILY FACE MASK

But it did give me an idea: would this be a clever way of DISTRACTING PEOPLE from bad news? Maybe even a possibility of 'BENDING' the news so that it appears more favourable to our position? There is an obvious danger in this, in that we're giving different news to deaf people. Somebody at some stage is likely to tell them that they're getting a version of events that is not the same as the one that people who are not deaf are receiving. Hmm . . . I think there is something in this, though. There might be a way of making it work.

Distract with visual noise.

BLOGPOST: SCHOOLS CLOSURE

Very, very bad news in many of today's newspapers. Sample headline:

STAYING AT HOME MAKES KIDS BRIGHTER

What the hell is this about? I'm furious. First paragraph:

A SOON-TO-BE-RELEASED report will make grim reading for Boris Johnson and Education Secretary Gavin Williamson. The study, which was compiled last week, shows that since schools closed in the UK on 23 March, pupils' cognitive abilities, including problem-solving skills, vocabulary, numeracy and literacy have all improved.

What?! It continues:

EDUCATOIN!
EDUCATOIN!
EDUCATOIN!

Rather than harming children's education, staying away from teachers and lessons seems to have boosted their performances in almost all key areas. In a random sample, three thousand children from England and Wales were evaluated on criterion-referenced and norm-referenced assessments. The Prime Minister's special adviser Dominic Cummings will be especially enraged by this report, as he has prioritised education and placed it at the top of the government's agenda.

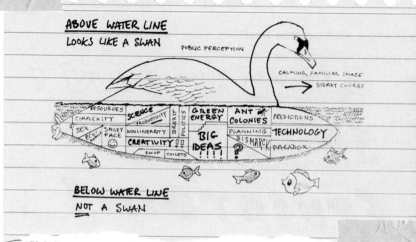

ABOVE WATER LINE
LOOKS LIKE A SWAN

PUBLIC PERCEPTION

CALMING, FAMILIAR IMAGE
STEADY COURSE

RESOURCES
COMPLEXITY
SEX ECONOMY
SMILEY FACE
SCIENCE
PRODUCTIVITY
NONLINEARITY
CREATIVITY
BREXIT
POLITICS
GREEN ENERGY
ANT COLONIES
BIG IDEAS !!!
PLANNING
BISMARCK
?
PREDICTIONS
TECHNOLOGY
PARADOX
SHOP
TOILETS

BELOW WATER LINE
NOT A SWAN

So this basically means that kids are better off not going to school. What has happened here? Called Williamson in and he really doesn't know what all this is about either. I really felt like sacking him, even though it's not his fault. To manufacture a monumental fuck-up like this would take years and he's only been in the job a few months. (I don't think it's Gove's fault, either, as I was watching him like a hawk when we were in the department together, and he mostly did what I said.)* Boris was away with his new kid, so I didn't bother trying to get him in on the meeting. (Anyway, he has absolutely no interest in education.) We (the government) have spent all our time since lockdown saying that, the longer schools are closed, the more damaging it will be to children's long-term prospects. Now it seems the opposite

* The roots of this must go back years. Blair, obviously.

is the case. Kids become smarter if they don't go to school. Williamson was at a loss as to what to do about this. 'What's the way forward, boss?' he moaned. (I knew that he didn't have any ideas.) I bet he's worried that if we close all the schools (not a plan actually proposed in the report, but I think it's strongly suggested) he might be out of a job. I have written about four hundred blogs about education, with all kinds of plans (illustrated by graphs) and clever ideas, and now this bombshell. This is worse than COVID-19. Fuck everything about this. I'll set up an independent inquiry within the party and then knock a few heads together.

<table>
<tr><td>20/06
2020</td><td>**WAR DIARY**</td></tr>
</table>

* Although if we've learnt anything from this disaster it's that scientists don't know much about science either and are clearly making it all up as they go along.

Well, well, well . . . The press goes mad over my trip to Durham while TODAY thousands of people congregate for a Black Lives Matter protest in London, and absolutely EVERYBODY who condemned me thinks THIS IS JUST GREAT. I'm no scientist,* as people are very quick to point out, but I think me and my small family going for a drive in my car would probably be less likely to spread disease than thousands congregating together, clearly breaking the law on a MASSIVE SCALE and not bothering at all with social distancing.

I'm struggling to think of a greater example of HYPOCRISY in history but I literally CANNOT THINK OF ANY!**

Had a chat with Boris about the whole BLM situation that is sweeping the world. Premier League footballers have recently 'taken the knee' and have 'Black Lives Matter' printed on their shirts. People have donated millions of pounds to the organisation. I've even heard that, at a Ku Klux Klan meeting held at the weekend, clan members had Black Lives Matter badges pinned on the back of their hoods.

** I'm leaving out the situation of me driving back to London while suffering two bouts of blindness, but I genuinely didn't think this was in any way dangerous.

Obviously everyone in the BBC and the rest of the media thinks that Boris is a racist because he's posh and went to Eton. Actually, the truth is he wants to please everybody and can't stand the fact that so many people utterly hate him. In fact, racism is on the way out in the Tory Party, and I would say that, nowadays, only seventy-five or eighty per cent of the members are genuine racists.*** However, Bojo will do almost anything to be popular, which is probably why he said to me:

'Maybe we should disband the police?'

'Really? Are you serious?'

'They're thinking about that in America, aren't they? The BLM people would love it, and it would prove that I'm not a racist.'

*** See blogpost from 12 September 2019: 'RACISM IN THE TORY PARTY'.

I explained to him that I thought it would be a mistake to disband the police in Britain. For a start, they're unarmed and hardly kill anybody. Of course, there are bad apples in the police force who are just bastards, and some people who just love killing other people. But that's true of any group of people anywhere.**** He then made the financial argument: 'We would save a hell of a lot of money if we didn't have a police force.' I agreed with him on that point, then extended the argument to other services that the government is responsible for: the NHS, unemployment benefit, transport systems, education, etc.

**** Especially Northern Ireland.

If we closed all those down, we'd have even more money. Boris shot back with: 'Well, that report that was in the papers yesterday . . .' (I was disappointed he'd seen it, as I'd tried to hide all of yesterday's newspapers from him.) '. . . it says that education makes little difference in a child's development, and I agree. The only thing I learnt at school was to read and write, and I probably would have picked that up anyway. So we could definitely get rid of education.' I could tell at this point that he was 'losing it' big time. I think the virus may have affected his brain more than anybody thought at the time, except me.***** Maybe he's not having enough sex? Could be a possibility that, with a small child running around, he just doesn't have the time. I'll see how he is over the next few weeks, but if it continues like this,

***** See War Diary of 5 May 2020.

HE'LL HAVE TO GO.

Given that everything here is
so fucked up, maybe we need to
rethink the Brexit thing.

WAR DIARY

Fuckin' 'ell – when will this war ever end? COVID-19 is still with us. Maybe it will be like Communism – around for seventy-five years before people get sick of it and move on to something else. Nobody has yet come up with a vaccine, and if Miley Cyrus or Lee Mack had been in charge of the World Health Organization we'd probably still be in more or less the same position we find ourselves now re: battling the pandemic. I had a chemistry set as a child – maybe I could have a go at coming up with a vax? If I have any time at the weekend, I may have a crack at it.

Now – the fucking schools. They're supposed to be opening soon, but there's been a massive cock-up re: exam results. The little darlings' exams were cancelled before the summer, so we've had to come up with a way of giving them results without them taking any actual exams. What the hell to do? Boris said, 'I'll leave it up to you chaps' – meaning me and Williamson. (Then he snuck off.) Obviously Williamson, like in that old song by The Sweet, 'didn't have a clue what to do!', so I brought Gove into the

conversation via Zoom. (G seemed to be on holiday in Barbados or somewhere – which wouldn't look good – but it was just a fake tropical background he'd conjured up behind him with an app or something.) Various plans were proposed:

1. Use algorithms.
2. Let teachers decide pupils' grades.
3. Pull names of successful applicants for uni out of a hat.
4. A combination of the above three ideas.
5. A combination of the above four ideas.

A* C−

Tony Blair's vote-winning strategy for education was that everybody should be forced to go to university, whether they liked it or not. There was a time (from the thirteenth century until 1997) when the only criterion for getting you into uni was how able your father was to pay the fees, but those days are sadly gone. (How SIMPLE that would make things now!)

It was an unsatisfying meeting (during which Williamson and Gove both collapsed due to stress), so I told the two of them that I was going to take the rest of the day to do a lot of research on the subject, and that we would reconvene in the morning. But then, on my way home, I turned on the radio news to discover that Williamson had said that he'd go with the algorithm method. That was at one o'clock. By the time the news rolled around again at three, he said he'd changed his mind and that he'd let the teachers decide. It's not that Williamson specialises in U-turns, it's more like he's in a circle that revolves erratically, jerking clockwise and anticlockwise in a completely unpredictable and arbitrary fashion. With a U-turn, you go back; Williamson goes back, goes forward again, goes a little bit more forward, goes back, goes back a bit more, goes forward, goes back again . . . etc., etc., ad infinitum . . .

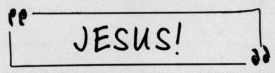

JESUS!

Sometimes I think I should just KILL them all: Boris, Williamson, even Gove . . . I know that they all love and admire me very much, but politics is a very tough game, and they would understand my reasoning if it was set out in purely tactical terms. I think it was

Hitler (in fact, it was definitely Hitler) who ordered the death of Ernst Röhm, the leader of the Nazi SA (Stormtroopers), when he felt that Röhm had outlived his usefulness. But it is wrong to see myself as a dictator. My role is to achieve my goals behind the scenes. I think I've actually done quite a good job, in my own modest, understated way – and I've done all this work while remaining largely anonymous. I propose once this COVID thing has passed, we clear out the 'dead wood' from the cabinet (i.e. everybody except Sunak) and get a new PM (because Boris has been basically shit). Then the future of the Conservatives can be a very bright one.

But at the moment ... I MEAN, FOR FUCK'S SAKE ...

CUMMINGS AS "EMPEROR NAPOLEON"

INDEX

Almighty, Christ: 8, 61; attitude to Brexit, 109

Ann, Ba, ba, ba, ba, Barbara (song by The Beach Boys): 18, 88; when sung backwards, harbours pro-Brexit message, 99

Bismarck, Otto von: DC's love of and devotion to, 6, 7, 8, 9–110, 111, 112, 113, 114–209; attitude to Brexit, 190

Bragg, Billy: 18; solidarity with miners, 78, 89, 90; takes Jacob Rees-Mogg hostage, 88; throws Colston statue into river and replaces it with one of John Peel, 200

Brasco, Donnie: 77; links to Mafia, 88, 90; involvement in Brexit campaign, 99–104

Castle, Barbara: 88; as Minister for Transport, 110

Castle, Barnard: 66

Cisco, San Fran (Be Sure to Wear Some Flowers in Your Hair) (song by Scott McKenzie; sung 'very out of tune' by Bill Cash to Quentin Letts at Brexit celebration party in January 2020): 99

Clarke, Ken: 55, 56; encounters DC in House of Commons bar, 77, 88; love of jazz, 88; disguises himself as pantomime horse in order to escape members of European Research Group, 109

Corbyn, Jeremy: 12, 56; agrees to allow IRA to store bombs in his flat, 37; hosts tea party for Hammas, 89; 'disgusting beard with the remnants of his breakfast still visible', 92; knifes to death armed assailant, 89; jealousy of Cilla Black, 98–112; visits to Cuba, 89, 103, 104, 107, 188, 189; experiments with invisibility leading to temporary insanity and deafness, 115; seen staring vacantly into pond in Hyde Park and 'looking morose', 116; final illness and death, 119

Cumberbatch, Benedict: 77; plays DC in Channel 4 Brexit comedy, 88; 'weird-looking bloke', 88; DC offered to portray in pantomime, 88

Cummings, Dominic: trip to Barnard Castle near Durham, 50; time in Russia, 67–229; as 'architect of lockdown', 77; *Top of the Pops* appearance as backing singer for Dexy's Midnight Runners, 55; advises Boris Johnson against wearing 'blackface' in Tory Party election broadcast, 66, 77; wishes Boris Johnson had died of COVID-19, 209, 210; designs beautiful earrings and jewellery based on ancient Persian prints, 99; earns Blue Peter badge as child, 77; provokes 'incident' on border between Russia and Chechnya leading to war, 89; joins celebrities on trip to India for TV programme *The Real Marigold Hotel*, 77; organises Live Aid and Band Aid with Sir Bob Geldof, 89, 99; designs COVID-19 commemorative coins and medals with his own face on them, 78; 'philosophy of politics', 88; difficulties with spatial awareness whilst doing jigsaw puzzles, 70, 75; illustrates children's book by David Walliams, 188; net worth of, 90; involved in mysterious yachting accident, 88; 'weird cough', 99; denies rumours that he invented COVID-19 pandemic in lab and released it to deflect attention from previous 'Brexit Bus' controversy, 18; co-writes *Mrs Brown's Boys*, 66; spends a year alone on desert island staring into space, 202; boosts Wi-Fi signal in cottage on parents' estate by installing second wireless cable router, 199; destroys memory stick containing secret Russian diaries, 200; mysterious knee pain, 201; cancels proposed trip to Venus, 202

Curtis, Ian: 56, 77; singer with Joy Division, 78; laments having to be in band which plays 'grim, oppressive music', 67; joins Showaddywaddy, 90; writes gags for Ken Dodd, 88, 99; attitude to Brexit, 108

Dekker, Desmond: 34; lyrics to the song 'The Israelites' misheard by Michael Heseltine, 67; and subsequent accusations of racism, 78, 79, 86; net worth of, 78

Dodd, Ken: 70; tax-avoidance allegations, 88; pop success in singles charts, employs Ian Curtis from Joy Division to write gags for him, 92; plays guitar on David Bowie's album *Low*, 99

Doe, a Deer, a Female Deer: 4; accusations of racism, 31

Dolly (the Sheep): 8; early experiments in cloning, 77; attitude to Brexit, 89

Duncan Smith, Iain: 55, 56; apology from Boris Johnson after BJ spells 'Iain Duncan Smith' as 'Ian Duncan Smith' in an article for *The Spectator*, 87; explains why his first name is spelt 'Iain' ('original Scottish spelling'), 78, 98; wears Nazi uniform at friend's party, 77; plays Scrabble with Jacob Rees-Mogg using only words that emerged or became popular during the COVID-19 crisis, 190

Far, a Long, Long Way to Run: 90

Farage, Nigel: and Brexit, 66, 90; origami demonstration, 88; purposely damages Subbuteo figures of German national football team to protest EU beef quotas, 102; whips Marcel Marceau lookalike on street, 89

Fear, Project: see Karloff, Boris

Ferguson, Dr Neil: 88, 98, 108; predicts end of the world 'on an unprecedented scale', 88; gives biology lessons to married woman, 110; wrong predictions of, 34, 35, 36, 77–89, 90, 111, 112, 113, 114, 115, 116, 117, 118, 119, 120, 121, 122, 123, 133, 134, 144, 145, 146, 147, 148; confusion with 'Niall Ferguson', 67, 68, 78, 79, 90, 91, 98–109, 110, 199

Ferguson, Niall: 44; confusion with 'Neil Ferguson', 67, 68, 78, 79, 90, 91, 98–109, 110, 199

Fire, (Goodness Gracious) Great Balls of: See Duncan Smith, Iain

Fox, Samantha: 77; regrets on going topless too early, 16; 'it's too early, isn't it?', 79; attitude to Brexit, 88

Francois, Mark: 'It ees bedtime, Francois. Please, when you 'ave finisheed pouring yourself zat cocktail, come and join me in ze . . . how you say? – chambre d'amour . . .', 56

George, Boy: 78, 90; comes to terms with his sexuality after watching David Bowie on *Top of the Pops*, 5; writes 'Karma Chameleon' while waiting in a queue for a stamp at the post office, opposes HS2 by tying himself to camel at protest meeting, 88; net worth of, 78; attitude to Brexit, 106; loses eighty-nine pounds in emergency diet, 101

General Election of 2019: 66, 77, 103; BBC's biased coverage of, 99, 208, 299; horse elected in Doncaster, 34; declared null and void, 67

Gove, Michael: 34, 35; throws monkey off bridge in Stockholm, 77; conspiracy theory about Malcolm Rifkind, 79

Hancock, Matt: 16, 89; peeling off un-postmarked stamp from postcard so that he can use it again, 99; wears nurse's uniform at friend's party, 77; defecates during cabinet meeting, 88; 'petrified of' DC, 99, 100, 101, 105–199, 200, 210–299, 300, 301, 301, 333; recruited by Russian intelligence, 345

Happiness, Walkin' Back to (song by Helen Shapiro): 18

Harry, Prince: paid forty billion a year by British taxpayers, 16; has enough of 'this shit' and fucks off to America with his attractive wife, 117

Hattersley, Roy: 77, 89; and perils of using facemask, 92; writes 50,000-page biography of Leo Sayer, 77

Hill, Bernard: see Castle, Barnard

Hitchens, Peter: 56, 78; creates own brand of peach-flavoured handwash to use during COVID-19 emergency, 32; chased through Oxford by angry mob, 88; does seven-thousand-piece jigsaw of Winchester Cathedral to pass the time during lockdown, 109

Hitler, Adolf: comparisons to Boris Johnson, 2, 4, 6, 7, 8, 9, 10, 11, 12, 20, 111, 112, 113, 114, 225, 116, 117, 118, 119, 120–122, 123, 124–440; and BBC bias, 16; attitude to Brexit, 17; wears Nazi uniform at friend's party, 77

Humperdinck, Engelbert: 77, 89; comment on comparison to Tom Jones: 'It's not unusual', 90; attitude to Brexit, 90; net worth of, 99

Johnson, Boris: 6; childhood, 15–75; 'blustering style of', 77; falls off roof and shatters stained-glass window after being chased by geese, 80; 'visibly erect' at function to announce Miss World beauty pageant, 88; disguises himself by wearing suit of armour and hiding in cupboard at Prue Leith's house, 99; relationship with DC, 101; extramarital affairs, 8, 9, 17–116, 117, 118, 119, 120–189, 190, 191, 192, 193, 194, 195–198, 200, 201–210, 215, 217, 218, 219, 220, 222, 234, 245, 246–260, 271, 272, 273, 274-275, 280, 281, 282, 284, 285, 286, 287, 189, 290, 300, 303, 310–328, 230, 332, 332, 332, 334, 335, 336, 337, 340–356, 360, 362, 363, 374, 440, 441, 442, 443, 445, 446, 447, 450–456, 458, 459, 460; attempts to poison Leo Varadkar, 88; rumours of his death, 99; recovers from COVID-19, 303; disappears forever leaving no trace, 309; in favour of fracking, 78; opposes fracking, 79; vacuuming obsession, 123, 289, 290, 300–401; speaks Latin to Meghan Markle, 90; compares rectangular hole in wall to letterbox, 67; net worth of, 78; trans controversy and 'bendy buses' remark, 83; recommends the best documentaries on Netflix to Jacob Rees-Mogg, 103; compares Muslims to a religious faith, 77; joins Instagram under assumed name 'Hector Surcheese', 89; promotes recycling, 19; and Windrush scandal, 88; procures saucer of milk for stray cat, 51;

edits *The Dandy* comic, 76; encounters difficulties whilst ordering pencils on Amazon, 90; parachutes into a skip full of burning tyres, 108; hoses himself down with washing-up liquid after an accidental meeting with Nick Griffin, 77; watches large log float ominously towards him while sitting in the sea at Broadstairs, 19; love of light aircraft, 88; love of light opera, 89; clothes washed up on beach, 44; apologises to Iain Duncan Smith after spelling 'Iain Duncan Smith' as 'Ian Duncan Smith' in an article for *The Spectator*, 104; rebukes members of British Embroidery Association, 12; recruited by Russian intelligence, 190; wears Nazi uniform at friend's party, 77; brain snaps into two pieces during meeting with Angela Merkel, 88; promotes third runway at Heathrow, 99; confuses Alan Yentob with Salman Rushdie, 45; confuses Salman Rushdie with Alan Yentob, 167; writes critical foreword for 1998 Australian reissue of *Mein Kampf* urging readers to keep the book 'in context', 109; taunted by 'who ate all the pies' chant at FA Cup Final, 89; warns against stockpiling of toilet paper during early days of COVID-19 crisis, 199; buys two hundred rolls of toilet paper during early days of COVID-19 crisis, 201; mends small hole in rucksack, 208

Jones, Owen: 23, 25; womb implant, 77; voluntary hysterectomy, 89; knits giant-sized national flag of Venezuela, 126

Karloff, Boris: see Fear, Project

Keane, Roy: 67, 72; rants for two hours about Lucozade and yoga after Manchester United defeat by Norwich City, 88

Kuenssberg, Laura: 65; and BBC bias, 89, 99; on everybody spelling her name wrong, 76; gives toy-bow-and-arrow demonstration outside Parliament to delighted audience of MPs' children, 705

Klansmann, Jürgen: founder of German Ku Klux Klan, 88

Klinsmann, Jürgen: former German footballer, 99

Klimt, Gustav: 80; attitude to Brexit, 66

Klopp, Jürgen: Liverpool manager, 85; net worth of, 78; warns against Brexit, 99; 'a nice guy, not like those other bastards', 109

Klumpt, Jürgen: condemns J. K. Rowling over transgender remarks, 97

Lineker, Gary: 'Releasing an animal like that on society is tantamount to surrendering every last vestige of decency left in the human race. I will track him down myself if I have to, and by God in heaven, I expect every man here to follow me through the gates of hell', 77; and BBC bias, 89

Livingstone, Ken: 55; exports live newts to Iran, 78

Lockdown, The: 7

Love, Geoff & His Orchestra: 78, 90, 99, 54; differences over Brexit, 56

'Lowdown' (song by Boz Scaggs): see Scaggs, Boz

Lynn, Vera: 103

M., Boney: see Rasputin, Ra, Ra, Lover of the Russian Queen

Maitlis, Emily: 67, 90; surname similar to 'weightless', 99; surname similar to 'waitress', 190; invited to present Academy Awards, 77; and BBC bias, 88; net worth of, 78

Mantel, Hilary: 77; does Henry VIII-themed crossword in record time, 90; wears Tudor costume at friend's party, 78

Markle, Meghan: 8, 77; chased by Prince Philip, a pack of dogs and an angry mob wielding sticks through Windsor Safari Park, 77; has enough of 'this shit' and fucks off back to America, 115

Masks, Face: see Ranger, The Lone

Mason, Paul: 55; as Marxist financial editor for the BBC, 78, 88, 99; as Marxist financial editor for *Channel 4 News*, 109, 110, 178; love of Northern Soul music, 144; skiing accident involving Diana Ross, 148; net worth of, 78; becomes trapped in goldfish bowl with angry fish but survives by breathing through straw until help arrives, 190

May, Theresa: 66; becomes Prime Minister, 88; suspect in Salisbury poisoning of Sergei and Yulia Skripal, 98; 'A devious and cunning criminal. She had the motive and the method to carry out these cruel attacks. The evidence is mounting, and I shall not give up on this' (assessment by ex-England rugby captain, Bill Beaumont), 77; abducted by UFO, 90; wears Nazi uniform at friend's party, 77

Me, a Name I Call Myself: 38

Miranda, Carmen: 88, 90; and 'cultural appropriation', 77; attitude to Brexit, 101

Moore, Charles: 77, 99; as editor of *The Spectator*, 88, 106, 109; marriage to Courtney Love, 99

Morrison, Van: 70; does voice-over for Carphone Warehouse, 99; attitude to Brexit, 100; recruited by Russian intelligence, 101

McDonnell, John: 88; Commander of South Down IRA, 88, 99,

106; explosives hidden in tent at Glastonbury, 99; digs twenty-mile-long tunnel under Long Kesh prison, 99; interned by British without trial, 88; blows up Loyalist chicken farm, 109; deputy leader of Labour Party, 119, 220, 230–256

Osmond, 'Little' Jimmy: 'Not so little any more', 88, 90; attitude to Brexit, 209

Pacino, Al: 78, 80; lands role in *The Godfather*, 90; attitude to Brexit, 190

Packham, Chris: as animal-rights activist, 60; hides endangered owls in his bedroom, 66; attitude to Brexit, 88; assassination attempt on DC, 109

Patel, Priti: 7; early life, 9–12; as professional dog-walker in Afghanistan, 88; time as Bond Girl, 90; opposes face masks, 98; digs 'average-sized' hole in garden, 101

Perry, Grayson: pottery-making technique, 77; becomes beloved by British public during lockdown, 88; knighthood, 109

Philip, Prince (Duke of Edinburgh): 8, 77; chases Meghan Markle through Windsor Safari Park accompanied by a pack of dogs and an angry mob wielding sticks, 77; wears Queen's dress at friend's party, 108

Potter, Beatrix: see Perry, Grayson

Potter, Dennis: see Perry, Grayson

Potter, Harry: see Perry, Grayson

Queen, The: 88, 92, 106; recruited by Russian intelligence, 209

Raab, Dominic: 77; takes over from Boris Johnson during PM's coronavirus infection, 88; eats live bat to prove that he can't contract COVID-19 from it, 89; wears Duke of Wellington uniform at friend's party, 77, 90; throws fake, but lifelike, cow at Keir Starmer, 88; recruited by Russian intelligence, 89

Ranger, The Lone: 8, 65; gives DC face mask advice, 90

Ray, a Drop of Golden Sun: 67

Rasputin, Ra, Ra, Lover of the Russian Queen (Boney M. song): 77; comparisons to DC, 88, 104

Red Wall, The: 'To get the ball into the net from that angle is just incredible. But you have to ask – what's happened to the wall? Luke Shaw has gone missing. And De Gea will be disappointed he hasn't covered it.' For 'Red Wall', a term used in UK politics to describe a set of constituencies in the north of England which historically tended to support the Labour Party, see 'General Election of 2019'

Rees-Mogg, Jacob: 78, 98; makes controversial remark about the Chinese, 66; as roadie for Slade, 88–98; ticks off waiter in restaurant after soup is served at two degrees below room temperature, 99; goes on caravan holiday with DBC Pierre, 100; net worth of, 78; describes Cliff Richard as 'looking young for a man of eighty', 109; auditions for *The Book of Mormon*, 178; recruited by Russian intelligence, 203

Rees-Mogg, Helena Anne Beatrix Wentworth Fitzwilliam de Chair: 12; reported by Boris Johnson as 'wearing a dress made out of lilacs', 34

Richard, Cliff: 45; described by Jacob Rees-Mogg as 'looking good for a man of eighty', 22; finishes second at Eurovision Song Contest, 88; throws up and is hospitalised after seeing the Sex Pistols on *Top of the Pops*, 67; BBC and police raid his house in joint operation, 99; net worth of, 78; pickets Cuban Embassy over lack of airplay for his records, 97; throws bag of dead flies at Val Doonican, 101

Ripper, Jack the: 45; at 1888 Tory Party Conference, 98; condemns J. K. Rowling over transgender remarks, 76

Robson, Sir Bobby: 1; time as manager at PSV Eindhoven, 300–342; recruitment by Russian intelligence, 309

Scaggs, Boz: 7; attitude to Brexit, 78

Sedaka, Sam-Neill: co-writes (with Bill Cash) rousing 'We're Out of Fucking Europe, So Time to Celebrate' song for Vote Leave, the political grouping designated by the Electoral Commission as the official campaign in favour of leaving the European Union in the Brexit referendum, 99

Sex: see Johnson, Boris

Shergar (horse): 66; disappearance of, 67; subsequent reappearance in kitchen of William Hague's country house, 109; condemns J. K. Rowling over transgender remarks, 145

Sinatra, Frank: *Ol' Blue Eyes is Back*, 77; attitude to Brexit, aversion to euro, 109; and BBC bias, 198

Simon, Paul: *Still Crazy After All These Years*, 107; attitude to Brexit, 110

Sirieix, Fred: 77, 89; 'not actually French' (accusation by Jürgen Klopp), 88

Slinky 'Mal' Malinki (Toby Young's dog): 77

Starmer, Keir: 77, 90; jumps over fence to steal apples from orchard beside Buckingham Palace, 50; wears Nazi uniform at friend's party, 77

Stiltskin, Rumpel: 70; attitude to Brexit, 75; condemns J. K. Rowling over transgender remarks, 88; net worth of, 100

Stürmer, Der (Nazi propaganda magazine): 77; attitude to Brexit, 89; condemns J. K. Rowling over transgender remarks, 65

Sturgeon, Nicola: 77; programmed by robots to do exactly as they say, 77; abolishes democracy in Scotland, 82; pushes washed-up whale on beach at Mull of Kintyre back into the water, 99; condemns J. K. Rowling over transgender remarks, 87; wears Nazi uniform at friend's party, 77, writes recipe book using only non-English ingredients, 109

Theroux, Louis: 66, 72; discovered doing low-key commentary at end of Prime Minister's bed as PM and girlfriend are making love, 77; popularity of, 79; hides in Jimmy Savile's wardrobe and tries on Savile's mother's dresses, 89; unloads unwanted electrical goods on country road near Chorley, 100; and subsequently fined, 101; marriage to Christine Hamilton, 218; recruited by Russian intelligence, 220

Trump, Donald: 55; founds Stiff Records, 77; comes up with slogan 'If It Ain't Stiff, It Ain't Worth a Fuck', 79; friendship with Jake Riviera, 90; 'weird orange colour', 77, 98

Varadkar, Leo: 66, lifelike duck impressions, 88

Virus, Corona the: 'worst threat to Britain since Second World War', 32; 'no worse than seasonal flu', 33

Wardrobe, The Lion, the Witch and the: 54; differences over Brexit, 56

Wark, Kirsty: 'sounds a bit like thirsty work', 99

Wayne, John: 77; appearance on *Parkinson* chat show, 79; attitude to Brexit, 78, 90

What Do You Want to Make Those Eyes at Me For? (song by Shakin' Stevens): 77, 81; used as campaign song for Sinn Féin during 2019 General Election, 87; and sung by Gerry Adams, Jeremy Corbyn and John McDonnell on SF election bus, 109

Wicks, Joe (the annoying workout guy): fitness techniques, 77; DC's father watches 'Workout for Seniors' on YouTube, 80; becomes beloved by British public during lockdown, 88; knighthood, 109

Widdecombe, Ann: 55; accidentally knocks over sixty-foot-high statue of Margaret Thatcher in Albania, 88; sells her house and furniture to fund Extinction Rebellion march, 93; presents *Naked Attraction* TV show, 101; wears Nazi uniform at friend's party, 77; rides donkey to victory in Conservative Party donkey derby fundraising event, 89; and subsequent disqualification, 99

Wind, The: 'blustering style of', 10

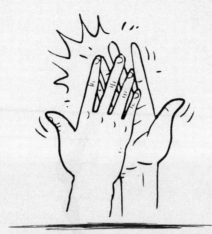

CLAP FOR CUMMINGS